Taken by Two Prison Guards

Taken, Volume 14

Jasmine Black

Published by Spunky Girl Publishing, 2022.

Also by Jasmine Black

Taken by Two Elves

Standalone
Shared Boxed Set

Taken by Two Prison Guards

Jasmine Black

Twenty-three-year-old Madeline "Mad" Madison has quite the temper. She got ten to life in prison due to her getting mad at her late boyfriend and there's only one way she knows of to keep herself calm and she's not getting *that* type of rehabilitation in prison. That is, until she's assigned hard labor and taken by two naughty prison guards.

Other stories by Jasmine Black include:

Taken by Two Doctors, Taken by Three Doctors, Taken by Two Bikers, Taken by Three Bikers, Taken by Two Billionaires, Taken by Three Billionaires, Taken by Two Bosses, Taken by Two Cowboys, Taken by Three Cowboys, Taken by Two Firefighters, Taken by Two Carpenters, Taken by Two Personal Trainers, Taken by Two Santas, Taken by Two Elves, Taken by Three Bodyguards, Taken by Two Cops, Taken by Two Prison Guards, Taken by Two Lifeguards, Taken by Two Mountain Men and more!

Copyright

Author Note

This is a work of fiction. Characters, places, settings, and events presented in this book are purely of the author's imagination and bear no resemblance to any actual person, living or dead or to any actual events, places, and/or settings.

Chapter One

"Hey, Mad. Get your ass out here! You're on the chain gang today."

Wow! I couldn't believe what I was hearing. I'd applied for work on the chain gang months ago and I was finally in!

Quickly I stepped to my prison cell door, which was all shiny gray metal and I slid my hands out the slot so he could shackle my wrists.

I'd been in solitary confinement for a month because once again my temper had gotten me into trouble, but I just couldn't keep calm when my rights were being trampled on, especially when it came to food.

I'd demanded my fair share of vegetables that particular day and when I was told they were out of vegetables, I'd lost it on the bitch behind me in the line up who'd told me to get over it and get a move on. I'd put her in the infirmary with a broken nose and a concussion. Too bad I had to learn the hard way there were no rights in here for prisoners, even for the ones, like me, who took no shit from anyone.

"You're in for some hard labor, Mad. Heard talk that you'll be raking leaves out of the ditches all day," Officer Myers said as he looked through the small bullet proof Peeping Tom window at me. He had short cropped red hair with matching freckles and pimples, along with a smirk on his face, but that didn't bother me much. I didn't care about hard labor. I just wanted to get out of this freaking isolation, the penitentiary and into the fresh air, even if it was to work my ass off.

My cell door slid open and he instructed me to walk ahead of him down the hall. We passed through several units, each one having locked doors that slid open when Officer Myers spoke into his breast mike. And then he directed me into a small room where seven other lady inmates were seated along a wall on a bench.

All of them looked mean and pissed off when they saw me walk in. I didn't recognize any of them. They must be from the other Blocks. So I just ignored them.

Besides, they were ugly older bitches and I didn't know why they were all frowning. They should be grateful to get to the other side of that twenty-foot-high cinder block wall topped with razor barbed wire.

"Okay ladies, there are your boots and gloves. Get those orange jumpsuits on over your clothes. Pick what fits you the best. Leave your shit on those shelves over there. After you're done, line up here for your leg shackles." A bored looking bald guy said from the other side of an open doorway.

He was pointing to a really long shelf lined with folded orange suits, work boots and gloves and then he pointed to another shelf that was a quarter full of other people's shoes. I figured those shoes belonged to ladies from other chain gangs that had already gone out this morning.

The women grumbled as we all stood and headed to the shelves. I removed my shoes, slipped into a jumpsuit that fit relatively well, then tried on a couple of pairs of boots until I found a comfortable size then put them on. I grabbed a tattered soft pair of work gloves and joined the other ladies in the line. I was at the end of the line, but I didn't care. I was getting the hell out of here for the day.

Had I thought I'd be doing hard time in a freaking prison for killing my boyfriend, I would have simply made myself disappear before I'd accidentally, or maybe not so accidentally, killed him.

But hey, in my opinion, the women of the world were better off without that piece of shit. I clamped down on my anger at thinking about him and watched as the guard handed me shackles for my ankles. I put them on, the clinking sounds of the heavy chains on my wrists and now my ankles irritated me.

Oh great. I couldn't even pick my nose without the chains making a racket. And so much for trying to make a run for it.

"Don't look so fucking down, prisoner. You're pretty enough. I'm sure you'll come back all smiles, especially on your first day." The old bitch of about fifty, who stood in front of me, muttered over her shoulder as she frowned and stared me up and down.

"Fuck off," I whispered.

She chuckled. "You're a live one, aren't you. The guards like the rowdy young girls. They'll have some fun with you."

It was my turn to frown as I wondered what she meant by her remarks.

The clinking of everyone's chains grated on my nerves as we were ushered down a hall into a large garage containing many prison vehicles and then we were guided onto a waiting prison van.

But I forced myself to stay calm and gaze out the window as the van started to move out of the garage and into the sunny day.

Five years I'd been here. Five years since I'd been in a vehicle.

Fuck, it was great feeling the sunshine beating on my face as it streamed past the thick-paned windows. I closed my eyes and remembered how I'd gotten here.

It had been a sunny autumn morning just like this one. I had once again been hoovered back into resuming a relationship with my on again, off again, boyfriend, Dane, who kept dumping me and then coming back.

During our time together, he'd gone from Mr. Jekyll to Mr. Hyde and back to Mr. Jekyll again. He'd been like a freaking seesaw and I never knew what mood he'd be in from one minute to the next. I'd get red-hot angry at him for his behavior and he'd say let's have sex to calm you down. So we did and I'd always feel better after a good roll in the hay.

As the relationship progressed he'd started blaming me for all his wrongdoings. Accusing me of sleeping around yet I found out he was the one screwing around. Then he'd started hitting me and then he'd blame me saying I had forced him to do it because of *my* anger.

Over the months I'd known him, he'd broken my jaw, my arms, ribs, fingers, and I couldn't name it all. To this day, healed body parts still ached.

Every time he left me; he'd come back a changed man. Romancing me with dates at expensive restaurants and professing his eternal love to me and that he was a changed man because of me. For some crazy insane reason I thought this last time he would stay Mr. Nice guy.

I was wrong. Again.

We'd had great sex that last night together, to "calm me down" because I'd been so angry at him for leaving in the first place. We always had great sex but I had come to realize over the years of incarceration, that's all we'd had.

Every other thing about him was no good. He'd been a virus that had tapped into my abandonment issues, he'd screwed with my head and used me for a place to stay and of course for sex.

When I had first met him, I'd ignored that gut instinct telling me he was all wrong for me. But he had love bombed me right at the beginning, wining and dining me, bringing me flowers and telling me everything I'd wanted to hear. That he'd loved me at first sight. I'd been on cloud nine, feeling like this was the man of my dreams. He'd been perfect. Or so I'd thought.

He told me he'd never hurt me like my last boyfriend had done. Rex had ghosted me, breaking off our relationship without so much as a reason. Dane said he'd never abandon me like my father had done when I was a kid. On and on he'd gone with his fake promises.

Instead of listening to my gut instinct and insist we take it slow and that I shouldn't be answering all of his prying questions so soon, I'd thought he was seriously interested in me. I'd swallowed his I love you bullshit hook, line and sinker and I'd let him into my heart and into my bed way too soon. He'd bedded me on our second date and had moved into my apartment within a week of us meeting at a bar.

Before I knew it, he'd begun to control me and isolate me from my family and friends. He'd come up with all kinds of excuses of why the two of us should be spending the evening together in bed having great sex instead of my going to my mom's birthday party or a friend's baby shower or whatever was going on that particular night.

Or he would conveniently get sick when I was supposed to go on a weekend getaway with my girlfriends. Or he'd harp on about how he couldn't stand my little sister and preferred it if the two of us go on a trip together conveniently every time Donna would be in town visiting my mom and wanted to swing by and see me too.

It had happened so slowly, this controlling and isolation, that I hadn't realized how bad it had gotten until I was hooked on him to the point I was terrified to break it off.

Finally I'd connected in my head that something was really wrong when I'd accidentally dropped my cell phone into the toilet at work where I was a receptionist for an electronics company. Of course, the phone had been fried. I'd been in such a panic, rushing to the office landline phone to call him asking his permission to go for a shit so he knew where I was in case I missed a phone call or a text from him asking what I was doing.

But I'd let my fears slide because I didn't want to displease him. Didn't want him to abandon me.

But he'd done it anyway. He'd begun ghosting me. Disappearing for days on end. Of course, that triggered my abandonment issues, making me try even harder to please him every time he came back from who knows where.

Yeah I was so hooked into that toxic bastard's abuse, it wasn't even funny.

Unfortunately for me, that addiction to him had been my downfall.

Chapter Two

That sunny autumn morning, after a wild night of make-up sex, which had calmed me right down, as it always did, he'd said he was leaving me for some other woman. Again.

I'd been so hurt and desperate and angry. We'd stood in the apartment hallway as I'd literally screamed I would kill him if he left me.

As he tried to go down the stairs, I'd grabbed his arm.

He'd laughed in my face; told me I was a stupid cow for ever believing that he loved me and then he yanked his arm free. He'd lost his balance, fell down a flight of stairs and broke his neck.

I'd heard the crack, ominous and loud. I can still hear that crack sometimes when I have nightmares about it.

Someone called the cops. Neighbors told them I'd been screaming, shouting, and threatening to kill him. One of them said she'd seen me push him down the stairs. Maybe from her angle, that's what she'd thought. Later I learned he'd been fucking that woman behind my back and that he'd told her I was a crazy woman.

So yeah, because of her testimony I wasn't a hundred percent sure I hadn't pushed him. I might have. It had happened so fast. A shitty pro bono lawyer had gotten me aggravated manslaughter and I'd landed in prison doing ten to who knew how long.

Shit happens, was the last thing my sister said when we'd hugged goodbye before I'd come out here. I'd told her not to visit and to go on with her life and not look back.

She hadn't visited and not once did I hear from her but I was glad she'd gone on with her life.

But my mom wrote letters and sent pictures. Donna was now married to some nice guy who worked as a taxi driver and they had two little girls with another girl on the way.

But then mom had up and died on me. Some rare brain cancer. A friend had written me a letter to let me know that within two weeks of her diagnosis, she was gone. No funeral due to the Covid pandemic. So yeah, shit happens.

As so many other times over the last years, I found myself thinking my life would have been so different had the apartment building elevators not been out of order that day, he wouldn't have taken the stairs and life would have been so much better had I never met the skunk.

I must have dozed off in the lure of the warm sunshine because when the van hit an exceptionally big bump, I opened my eyes to find we were in the countryside now. Huge towering trees lined both sides of the gravel road on which we were travelling. Bright yellow, orange and crimson red leaves were swirling down like a colorful snowstorm as the wind blew against the tree branches.

The scenery was really pretty.

I smiled. Probably for the first time in five years.

I watched as we passed a chain gang. The women were wearing bright orange jumpsuits just like the ones we wore. They were raking leaves in deep ditches. They didn't look happy. Not one of them looked up, nor did anyone wave.

Beyond the trees and ditches, farmland stretched out everywhere. Some pastures were filled with golden bales of hay and other pastures had fluttering yellowing corn stalks or bright orange pumpkins splayed out upon the ground.

The driver of the van turned off the gravel road and kept driving along a rutted trail that had seen better days.

Up ahead was another vehicle. A white van similar to this one, with the words of our prison on it.

"Oh look, the welcoming committee is here." That same woman who'd spoken to me earlier muttered from the seat behind me.

She didn't sound cheerful.

"They must have gotten word there's fresh flesh in this gang. They're gonna try her out," replied an older woman sitting on the bench seat across the aisle from me.

She turned to look at me and my tummy dipped like I was on a roller coaster.

"Aren't you the lucky one," she said in a low tone.

She suddenly smiled at me and wiggled her white eyebrows. She only had one tooth in her mouth and she looked like a creepy old witch.

Man, I hoped I didn't look like her when I got that old.

The van stopped. The door opened.

"Alright, Madeline Madison. You get out here. The rest of you ladies stay seated. You'll be coming with me."

There were a couple of snickers from the women and then silence.

I swallowed as uneasiness whipped through me.

I was to go out there with those two prison guards? On my own?

Reluctantly I stood and peered out the window trying to see where the chain gang might be out here in the middle of nowhere. I saw nothing but a large field filled with orange pumpkins and the two male prison guards standing by their vehicle.

"Come on, Mad! Get a move on! Daylight is burning!" the van driver shouted. He sounded irritated.

My chains clinked like crazy as I hobbled down the aisle of the van. All the ladies were as quiet as church mice and looked the other way as I passed them. They all wore frowns. Kind of like they were pissed off.

Oh my gosh! Was I getting preferential treatment because it was my first day? Were they jealous?

I shook my head at that crazy idea.

My uneasiness vanished when I stepped out of the van and felt the crisp cool October air whipping against my face.

I was free. Well, sort of.

I held my breath as I stood there and sized up the two prison guards.

They wore identical uniforms. Dark blue shirts and tan pants. Shiny black boots, and dark blue baseball style hats with the words Prison Guards emblazoned in white lettering across the front. The two men were cute and well built. Wide shoulders. Slender hips and long legs.

Something hummed to life inside of me when I spied bold erections pressing against their pants.

But they wore lots of weapons.

Each man wore what I called a beating stick. They each had a holstered gun on their belt too. There was mace, tasers, handcuffs and walkie talkies.

These guys looked like serious business. Once again the thought of escaping seemed out of the question.

When I looked up into the faces of the two tall prison guards, alarm bells went off, but in a really enjoyable way. Each guard had a predatory look in his eyes and I sensed I was their sexual prey. I wasn't sure at the moment if I might just be fantasizing, but my pussy was clenching and creaming hot liquid like it hadn't done in quite a few years and my nipples suddenly seemed bigger as they pressed against my bra, aching to be free.

Suddenly I got the feeling this wasn't going to be a regular day of hard labour, at least not in the traditional chain gang sense.

I blew out a tense breath as the van filled with my fellow inmates drove away.

"Good morning, officers," I said politely.

Just because they owned me here in the prison system didn't mean I had to be a bitch. Besides, I always found you get more of what you want if you blow honey at the guards. And I just wanted to be outside of the prison as much as possible and for as long as possible.

"Morning, "the tallest guard answered. He held a clipboard in his big hands.

"Just want to confirm you are Madeline Madison. In for aggravated manslaughter, ten years to life."

He looked up from his clipboard awaiting my answer.

I realized he had the most fabulous aqua blue eyes when the sun shone on them.

I nodded.

"I'm Officer Dixon and my partner is Officer Ashton. You're here to pick pumpkins. Follow us."

I found myself relaxing. For a few seconds there I'd fantasized about a menage a trois with these two men.

Bummer. I'd much rather be having red hot sex instead of picking freaking pumpkins.

Be careful what you wish for, a wary inner voice warned. I shrugged it off. Yeah, right, like in my wildest dreams.

I followed the two guards into a dense line of trees, fully expecting to find a gang of women working on the other side, but there was no one around. Just a field loaded with big fat orange pumpkins.

It kind of reminded me of the story of Cinderella and for a split second I wished I were her and one of those pumpkins would magically turn into a beautiful carriage and whisk me away from here to some faraway land and to my very own Prince Charming.

"Here. Use this to cut the stems." Officer Ashton broke into my fantasy.

He held out a utility knife and stood back as I took it. He had dark brown eyes and dark brown hair with a tiny ponytail that peeked out from the back of his hat.

He pointed down the field.

"Over there is the line of bins for you. Fill each one level to the top, then go to the next bin."

I spied a long line of wood slat bins. Had to be at least fifty of those containers and just one of me.

Lovely. It appeared I wasn't going to have an easy first day as I'd hoped a few minutes ago.

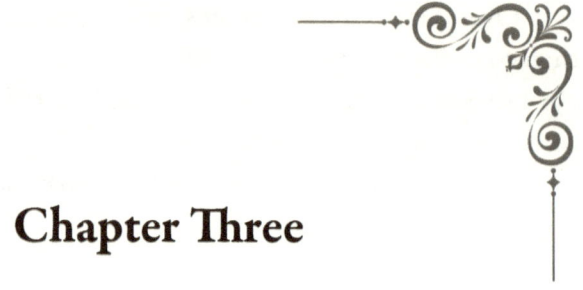

Chapter Three

I headed toward the nearest pumpkin, crouched, sliced into the stem, picked up the heavy orange fruit or vegetable or whatever the hell it was and walked to the bin.

"Handle them like eggs, please," Officer Dixon instructed. He held a pen to the clipboard and watched me.

"Or gently like a man's balls," the other officer chuckled.

I bent over, rolled my eyes at his comment and placed the pumpkin into the bin.

If these two officers had balls as big as these pumpkins they'd be in the field helping me and I was sure they wouldn't help because from my experience the guards were like ornaments. Standing around and looking pretty.

And so it went. The two guards watched me work from afar, studying me like I was some insect and I kind of ignored them. I was too busy slicing into pumpkin stems, breathing in the fresh air and languishing beneath the hot sun.

After awhile though, my shoulders were getting sore. So was my back, my thighs and my neck. The chains were rubbing my wrists and ankles something awful. I was also really getting hot being trapped in this orange jumpsuit, not to mention I was getting thirsty. But I knew it would be rough the first few days. Especially since I'd been lounging around like a prison princess the last five years.

So, I just ignored my owies and kept going until I heard a sharp whistle.

I stopped.

"Break time! Your box cutter stays there. Show me your movements as you place it and then come over here!" One of them shouted.

Cautiously I placed the cutter on the edge of the bin.

Like seriously here. They were armed to the teeth with weapons and I had chains on my wrists and ankles and they were afraid of me?

I reached the men. One of them handed me a nice big paper cup filled with ice cold water. I drank it like there was no tomorrow and I wished for another one. I wasn't offered seconds so I kept my mouth shut.

"Do you need to relieve yourself?" Officer cute blue eyes asked.

"No, sir."

"Sit down here on the ground. Relax, prisoner," he instructed.

I sat where he pointed. The ground was full of leaves, but damp and cold. Again, I said nothing as the wetness seeped against my behind.

"You've got a fifteen-minute break," Officer Dixon said.

I nodded and stared off into the distance watching a bunch of black crows circling around up in the sky. They were probably waiting me to drop dead and then start picking at my corpse while these two guards just stood around like the glorified decorations they were and watched.

I chuckled aloud at that thought, unable to stop myself.

"Something funny, Mad?" Officer Ashton asked.

"No, sir."

Officer Dixon was looking at his clipboard as he hovered over me.

"Your records show that you appear to be a very good prisoner. You have no problem following orders, except for some hiccups along the way due to your short temper. It seems to get you into trouble."

Just sticking up for myself, asshole. But I didn't dare say that aloud. He would think I was having an attitude and write me up.

"Yes, sir."

"Have you tried the anger management courses?" Ashton asked.

"Yes, sir."

"Not working from the latest solitary run, eh?" he asked.

"No, sir." I wished they would just shut the hell up. I wanted to listen to the wind rustling through the branches and pretend I was somewhere in a park or something.

"You appear to follow instructions easy enough this morning. Lots of girls would have already broke down and complained about something like a sore back, wanting out of their jumpsuits and chains or wanting to go back to the prison. But we can see that you're one of the tough girls," Officer Dixon complimented.

"I try, sir." For a brief moment, I felt proud. That is, until his next question.

"Aside from your temper, are you a submissive?"

I blinked as shock rolled over me. Had I just heard right? The prison guard had asked me if I was a submissive? Like in sexual terms?

I kept my eyes locked straight ahead, realizing that my first instinct about their predatory gazes and those erections had been correct. Now I understood the comments back on the van from those women. I was a lucky one, one of them had said. They must know what goes on out here. How come I hadn't heard about it?

"You're not answering my question. Are you a submissive?" Dixon asked again.

I swallowed at my suddenly dry throat. My heart was picking up speed and to my surprise, my pussy was quivering and growing hot.

"I'm not sure what you mean, sir?" I said tightly and kept my gaze on the circling crows in the field.

"Let me rephrase this. If we give you an extra fifteen-minute break, will you let us suckle your breasts?"

Heat fused through me at lightning speed. I began to tremble, in a really enjoyable way, as his words sank in.

Did they have a suckling fetish?

The idea of having two men's hungry mouths at my nipples hadn't even entered my mind. I inhaled deeply and took a moment to compose myself. I was a pretty fast thinker and I needed to spin this to my advantage.

"If you give me those extra fifteen minutes as alone time before you suckle at my breasts, then sure. But no bites and no hickeys," I said as I stared straight up at them. No way was I going to be having to explain myself in the shower room to the other women or to the nurse in the infirmary with infected bites on my breasts.

Both men grinned down at me, their faces transforming from seriousness to glee.

I had no problem noticing their erections were much bigger pressing against their pants now.

"Do you have trust issues?" Officer Dixon asked with a snicker.

"Let's just say I like to get paid ahead of time." I answered.

I was really getting tense. What if they decided to make a report on me if I didn't comply? I mean, I wouldn't mind having a little sexual fun and call me totally freaking insane, but the idea of these two men at my breasts was turning me on big time.

Huh, maybe I was the one with a suckling fetish?

"Just so we understand each other. What happens out here, doesn't get told back at the prison. It stays here." Officer Ashton's gaze had returned to one of seriousness again.

Like whom was I going to tell? I was a loner in the prison system and that was probably why I'd never heard of what went on out here. Up until today I'd just wanted to do my time and get the hell out.

"I understand," I said.

Both of them swore softly, and to my surprise, they walked away, leaving me alone. I blew out a nervous breath. What in the world had I been thinking agreeing to this?

Why was I feeling so flushed and so unbelievably aroused? Even my ass was getting in on the action, clenching up a storm as I envisioned one of them sliding his shaft into my anal canal.

Wow, over five years without sex sure did wreak havoc on me. At this point I was ready to say yes to anything they asked, even if it meant having them screwing my brains out in the field while those crows watched us. Anything so I didn't have to lift another heavy pumpkin.

So instead of having an enjoyable break, my imagination went wild as I waited for the two men to return. The break seemed endless, torturous.

Instinctively I knew they were just testing out the waters, so to speak, to see how compliant I might be. Or if I would run hysterically back to the prison crying rape.

By the time they returned, I was wound up so tight, I could barely think straight.

"Time's up," Officer Dixon said in a guttural voice.

"Have you changed your mind?" Officer Ashton asked. His voice was husky yet alert.

I shook my head.

"Good. Then stand," Ashton ordered.

I did as he instructed and stood in front of both of them. I noticed they'd removed their hats and their weapons were no longer on their belts.

Okay, this was interesting. No one had weapons, but still, there was two of them against one of me. And I had the chains hobbling my legs and wrists.

To my shock, Ashton produced a key.

"Unlock your wrist chains. I don't know about you, but the sound of those chains is grating on my nerves," he said.

"Try being in my shoes," I muttered.

I took the key.

I jammed the key into the wrist restraint. It popped open and the chains dropped onto the ground.

I wondered how he'd had the right key for my chains. Had this all been planned ahead of time? It surely seemed so.

Wow, it felt good to have my arms free from the heaviness of the metal. I handed him back the key and he shoved it into a breast pocket.

"Now unzip your jumper and let's get a nice closeup look at your breasts," came Officer Dixon's instruction.

Chapter Four

I guess I didn't move fast enough because he repeated himself.

"Unzip your jumper," Dixon said again.

I could see the heat flaring in the two men's eyes. Could feel an insane need to do their bidding. Maybe I *was* a submissive? I had never thought of myself as one, but maybe that's why I had been so easily duped into getting into bed with men in my past?

"If you insist," I said in as soft a voice as I could muster.

Unexpected excitement roared through me as the men watched my every move. I reached up and found my zipper, then slowly, ever so slowly, I pulled it down to my waist and smiled inwardly.

I was wearing a T-shirt underneath.

Disappointment flared in their eyes.

"Off with everything above your waist just like we agreed," Officer Ashton whispered.

"And no more games," Dixon said in a serious tone.

Hmm, had I frustrated them so easily? Having such power over these two prison guards was irresistibly amusing.

"I'm not sure what you mean," I teased.

I'd never been one to be embarrassed at being naked in front of a man. I'd always been comfortable in my own skin and being out of the prison walls, it almost felt like being free. I even felt playful.

"We are in charge. When we instruct you to do something, you will not play sexy. Is that understood?" Dixon growled.

Oh crap. For a moment, I *had* felt freedom sifting through me. Despite his warning, my mind was beginning to imagine all kinds of scenarios of getting them to do my bidding. But it appeared they wanted to remain in charge. At least for now.

My hands trembled as I slid my arms out of the jumpsuit. I couldn't resist continuing my slowness and I made sure to keep my movements seductive.

My mind was whirling with plans. If I could get these two men hooked on me, then I might be able to get more out of this than a mere extra fifteen-minute break.

I reached for the hem of my T-shirt, watching them carefully. Their eyes followed my every move with captive interest. The two men were truly thrilled, and so I lifted my shirt up and over my head. The only thing left was my bra.

"Go on," Officer Ashton prodded.

Both men had moved closer and stood directly in front of me.

I began to remove my bra, feeling both disbelief and some weird, electrified anticipation. My pussy was wet and I noticed their faces were flushing.

Suddenly, my swollen breasts spilled free and I stood tensely as the two guards stared.

"Wow, they were right. You do have magnificent big breasts. So juicy looking," Officer Dixon commented.

I stiffened. Okay, so who was *they*? His comment solidified my suspicions that this had all been set up. "Look at those luscious ruby red nipples," Ashton said.

"Like big red lollipops," the other replied.

Sexual arousal coursed through me at the intoxicating way these two men were ogling me. Desire raged in their eyes and I could literally see the tension tightening their bodies. Could feel the tension zipping through the air and wrapping around me.

"Just stand nice and still. No touching us under any circumstances," Officer Ashton whispered.

I gasped in surprise as both of them moved at the same time. They reached out, their hot hands quickly cupping my breasts. I cried out as their heads lowered and their heated mouths covered my nipples.

Their lips tugged on my sensitive flesh. Their tongues licked and lapped. Instinctively I arched my back, pushing my breasts harder against them needing a firmer contact.

I loved what they were doing to me. Understood at some primal level that this was a seduction.

My nipples grew hard and achy as they forcefully sucked. Intense heat fused throughout my body.

"One day we may even decide to make you pregnant, so we can get our daily intake of milk. Would you like that?" Dixon murmured around my quivering nipple and then took it right into his hot mouth again.

I couldn't believe what I was hearing and to my surprise a powerful surge of desire roared through me. I creamed at the thought of being pregnant. My belly swollen. My breasts heavy and ripe with milk for them to suckle.

Oh have mercy, the idea of it was turning me on so bad. I must have gone nuts in the prison system for such a suggestion to excite me. I'd never wanted kids. But now, suddenly, I did and I didn't even know these two men!

I watched them beneath dazed, half-lidded eyes as they sucked harder, their mouths tugging and bruising my tender nipples. The pulling created sensations that spiraled to my belly and then arrowed down between my thighs. My pussy felt heavy, hot and throbbed with need. The need to be taken by these two strangers.

I moaned, whimpered, and cried out as their large hands massaged my breasts and their hot lips forcibly tugged on my straining nipples. I was seriously creaming up a storm. My lower belly was tightening. My pussy was clenching. My breathing became fast.

A powerful surge of arousal lashed me as I imagined the two men sliding their cocks into me.

I swear I was about to orgasm. And then I *was* orgasming!

I shuddered within the uncontrollable spasms and moaned as my tender pussy muscles clenched on empty air. I became lost in ecstasy. Bucking and keening at the beautiful onslaught of convulsions.

Pleasure lashed through me like electrified whips. I knew I'd want more of this when it was over.

But all too soon my orgasm ebbed, leaving me panting as the two men drew their mouths away.

"Don't read too much into what I said about getting you pregnant. It was just in the heat of the moment," Dixon whispered. But from the lust shining in his eyes, I knew he was lying. I knew he had some sort of breast and lactating fetish.

I nodded jerkily.

For a few luxurious moments, I'd dreamed his craziness. And it was crazy. But pretending and play acting didn't hurt anyone.

"Break time is over. Back to work. Leave your breasts free for us to see and we'll keep your wrist restraints off, deal?" Dixon asked.

He was back to his serious attitude again.

I could protest. Hell, I should protest. At the very least I should bargain for some longer breaks if they wanted to see my breasts some more.

But I'd just had a damn good climax and I felt satiated. I wasn't in the mood for anything but following orders. Yet I seriously couldn't wait to see what else they wanted from me.

I adjusted my prison-issue jumper by securing the top part around my waist, tying the arms together and then I returned to working with the pumpkins, topless. I just loved having my wrists freed from the chains and having my breasts exposed to the fresh air and sunshine. My nipples ached from the prison guards forceful lips but I had the added bonus of them ogling me.

They couldn't get enough of watching me and I couldn't wait for them to suggest doing some other sexual activity with me. But I also realized I had to have patience. I didn't want to come across as desperate and that I actually craved more. If I did that, I'd lose the ability of bartering with them.

So, I waited for them to make their next move.

Lunch came and the guards presented me with the traditional prison food. Boring tasting sandwiches bottled water and a fruit cocktail in a small tin. I also noticed their weapons were back on their belts.

To my angst, they left me alone to eat, moving away down the treeline where I noticed they ate delicious looking extra large submarine sandwiches and steaming coffee from a Thermos.

They also remained serious for the rest of the day, standing or sitting like ornaments on the empty bins as they continued to watch me working topless. My big breasts jiggled as I lifted each heavy pumpkin into my sore arms. My nipples had grown ultra-sensitive due to their suckling and now with the sunlight beating down on them, they appeared redder than I'd ever seen them. I hoped I wasn't getting a sunburn there. I did, however, soothe them as I rubbed my hot, tender buds against the outer flesh of the cold pumpkins.

The prison guards never mentioned what had happened earlier and my thoughts continued to churn with ideas of how I could use their sexual interest in me to my benefit.

During my second break in the afternoon, the men instructed me to put on my bra and top. To my disappointment the chains came back on my wrists and I felt defeated.

About two hours later I was instructed to get into their prison van. Then they drove me back to the prison. Before I left the van,

Dixon muttered a see you tomorrow morning, which had excitement pummelling me.

Thankfully, I was put back into solitary confinement instead of general population. Here, in my cell, I spent the rest of my evening napping, doing some reading, playing solitaire on my laptop, eating supper and being alone with my naughty thoughts about how the two prison guards had suckled my nipples so intensely that I'd orgasmed. That had never happened to me before. Climaxing just because my nipples had been so hotly stimulated with their incredibly talented lips was something new and electrifying.

By bedtime I was so aroused at thinking about what Dixon and Ashton had done to me that I was ready for a good round of masturbating.

Lights dimmed at eleven and I waited for a little while. Finally, I heard the guard's footsteps pause in the hallway outside my cell. The little door on the Peeping Tom window slid open so he could look inside. He was doing a head count, making sure I hadn't escaped.

They did that throughout the night and it irritated me that my privacy was invaded on such a routine basis. But hey, I was in prison, so privacy was pretty much non-existent.

When I heard the little door slide back into place, I pushed the blanket off my naked body, lifted my knees and spread my legs wide.

Chapter Five

Then I let me imagination carry me away. My hands smoothed over my nipples and boy, they sure were tender. But I also realized the added tenderness gave my nipples an extra shot of pleasure pain when I touched them.

I imagined Dixon and Ashton's eager mouths at my breasts again. Their lips sensually tugging and sipping. Their tongues lusciously licking and lapping like it happened this morning.

I moaned softly as I gently pinched my nipples and massaged my heaving breasts, gasping as exquisite pleasure quickly sparked to life and whipped through me at my intimate touches.

The desire for an orgasm arrowed along to my lower belly and into my aching vagina. Just as it had this morning.

Eagerness pummeled me as I reached between my thighs and rubbed my fingers around and over my ultrasensitive clitoris. Then I dipped my digits into my vagina for some lube. I smoothed my wet fingers over my clit, tenderly massaging and then dipped into my vagina again.

Anticipation quickly erupted and I fought to remain in control as I stroked around my vagina and tugged at my pussy lips. My juices were spilling from me now and my body was tightening with awareness as I imagined Dixon and Ashton there at my breasts again.

I spread my thighs wider and stroked my palm over my lower belly, caressing my tight flesh and breathing through the erotic shivers of anticipation. Heat flayed my body as I continued to pinch my nipple and thrust two fingers in and out of my vagina. Then I withdrew and rubbed my swollen clitoris before pistoning my fingers into my vagina again, fuelling the inferno of need there.

My body tightened and my breaths grew harsh. Slurping sounds split the air as my fingers thrust faster. The pleasure shudders slammed into me, making me cry out at their intensity.

But I didn't care if the prison guards heard me as the convulsions embraced me like an invisible lover. Explosive pleasure whiplashed through my body, making me writhe like a shaking ragdoll. I twisted and bucked within the beautiful agony, holding onto the shudders for as long as I could until the pleasure disappeared, leaving me panting and perspiring.

Wow, that had been quite intense.

I closed my eyes and just lay there, naked and spent, not caring if a guard came by and checked up on me. Let them look.

Suddenly, I couldn't wait to get back to that pumpkin patch in the morning. To hell with bartering. I knew I would give the prison guards anything they wanted.

They were bastards. They had turned on my sexuality once again and I didn't want it to stop.

I smiled, closed my eyes and slept.

The next morning I was so ready to get back outside the prison walls and happily have some more sex with the two prison guards. To my surprise, I didn't ride back to the pumpkin patch with the other women of the chain gang like I did yesterday morning. Instead, I was instructed to hop into the van with officers Dixon and Ashton.

Both remained silent.

Dixon drove.

He kept peering at me in the rear-view mirror, which made me both uncomfortable and aroused.

Despite their silence, I sensed both men were quite tense with eagerness. Lust shone in their hot gazes and their wide shoulders seemed taut beneath their uniforms.

As we drove into the country, I soaked up the brilliant autumn colors. The bright blue sky, the auburn and crimson laden trees in the distance and the yellowing fields. We drove past a couple of chain gangs consisting of orange suited prison women who were raking the colorful leaves or collecting garbage in the ditches beside the same road I'd travelled yesterday. Soon we turned onto the gravel road and then the same farmer's lane.

The van came to a stop and the two officers jumped out.

My heart was beating a mile a minute as the van's side door slid open. Dixon stood there and he stared at me, saying nothing.

What was he thinking? Could he read my excitement? Or did he think they had gone too far with me yesterday and had decided to stop so they wouldn't get caught?

Oh, I hoped it was not the latter. I held my breath and waited for his next move.

"We have a proposal for you. We'll discuss it at first break. Out of the van. Time to work," he said.

Both frustration and exhilaration whirled through me as I stepped out of the van and into the fresh air and sunshine, my wrist and ankle chains clinking through the quiet air. To my surprise, Dixon removed my wrist restraints.

A moment later I was once again in the pumpkin patch, cutting thick stems and hauling the bright orange pumpkins to the wooden bins while the two ornaments watched and spoke with each other in hushed whispers.

By the time break arrived I was tired and so thirsty I downed the first huge paper cup of water that Ashton produced for me and then I had the nerve to ask for a second helping. Thankfully, I got no protest.

Dixon went to the van and returned with a second cup of delicious ice-cold water.

"Looks hard working out there alone, Mad. How would you feel if we helped you out until lunch?" Dixon asked.

"Suit yourself," I answered as I sat down on the ground.

Perspiration dripped from my forehead, my back ached, and my thighs were getting sore from all that squatting to pick up the heavy pumpkins. I was glad of the offer, but I wasn't getting my hopes up. From my experience prison guards just stood around looking for trouble.

"We know you like to get rewarded ahead of time." Dixon said.

He let his sentence hang in the air for a few seconds, and I was instantly alert.

"What do you propose?" I asked, trying very hard not to appear interested.

Hell, last night, before, during and after masturbating, I'd been ready to do anything they wanted but today after a good night sleep, I was back to thinking about what I would get out of this. It would be really stupid of me to give away free sex when I could get something in return.

"You'll also get an extra half hour for lunch," Ashton added.

"After you get that, you give us what we want," Dixon said in a cool tone.

"What's that?"

"To suck your nipples again for one. And your pussy," he replied.

My breath backed up in my lungs at this new request. My vagina clenched with wicked anticipation as I imagined having the two men going down on me.

I didn't say anything. Didn't want to appear eager, but I could hardly wait for it to happen.

"And to outfit you with a butt plug," Ashton added.

Shock reverberated through me. I continued to remain silent, realizing what was eventually going to happen. Anal sex and possibly a threesome in the near future. An awesome awareness blew through my body and my mind. This was too good to be true.

The two guards stared at me waiting for my answer. I could read the hunger in their eyes. Could feel their need zipping through the air between us. Could feel arousal slamming into me.

Just thinking about them seeing me entirely naked made me feel heady in a really nice way.

"I've got conditions," I hedged.

Dixon frowned. Ashton appeared eager though.

"An offer of assistance and extra lunch time isn't enough for you?" Dixon growled. He appeared angry, but I suspected it was all an act to keep me in line. I decided not to buckle.

"I want a proper lunch. No prison food. And this suckling needs to happen on a nice cozy blanket, like the one I saw in the van. I want a nice warm ass out of the deal."

Dixon chuckled.

"So, you want to be treated like a prison queen, instead of the lowly prisoner that you are."

"I am a queen," I stated firmly. "And if you want this to go any further then you will start to treat me like a queen out here. That means helping with the work all the time. And if you want to knock me up eventually and live out your pregnant woman fancies, then by all means knock me up."

I couldn't believe how bold I had gotten. I noticed the tips of Dixon's lips turn upward ever so slightly. I could tell he was barely keeping it together. I dropped my gaze to the area between his thighs and watched the big erection tent his pants.

Oh yeah, his pregnancy fetish was my hook, and I could tell Dixon was hooked as his eyes got so wide with excitement that I swear I could see the wheels turning inside his brain.

"I'll have to think on the pregnancy. Not sure if we'd be allowed around you if we got you pregnant."

"Then you'll have to make sure they don't find out, won't you?" I answered in a cool voice.

Wow, I really was going too far with this, wasn't I? But I would not allow myself to get pregnant, or would I? Maybe I would just play them for as long as I could. Maybe one day I'd have them wrapped so much around my little finger, they'd help me escape. Wouldn't that be something.

"Okay, we'll meet your conditions. After lunch, you belong to us," Dixon growled. His aqua blue eyes flashed with obvious enjoyment.

"But until then, we want you working topless out there with us. The scenery will get us in a really good mood," Ashton said.

I nodded, trying hard not to tremble from the awakening coursing like liquid fire through my veins. Yesterday I enjoyed having the two men watch my breasts. I also loved having my breasts free with the warm sunshine beating down on my tender nipples. Then I could soothe the achy need of imagining the men suckling at my nipples by rubbing my tender red buds against the cold pumpkins. I would do the same today.

"We have a deal," I replied.

As I unzipped my jumpsuit, I smiled inwardly as the two prison guards watched my every moment.

Chapter Six

S lowly, seductively, I slipped my arms out of the suit like I had done yesterday, and then I removed my top. A moment later, my bra was off and my big breasts spilled free of their restraints.

I could barely wait until after lunch when my lower half was just as free.

To my surprise the two prison guards labored quickly and efficiently. Neither spoke to me nor to each other as they sliced stems and carried the pumpkins to the bins.

When lunchtime rolled around, I was quite ready to skip it and go straight to the sex, but Dixon and Ashton were sticking to the agreement and produced a delicious looking fried chicken breast, some potato salad, a huge slice of French style bread and a sealed container of green salad along with some packets of French dressing. Plus a thermos of delicious black coffee.

Man, I was drooling just looking at this food. It surely was a feast fit for a queen and it was all displayed on that snug looking blanket I had requested from the back of the van.

I devoured the food, eating topless, ignoring the two prison guards as they watched me from afar. They ate quietly, and I knew they had given me a share of their lunch. But I didn't care.

The prison lunch would have been the same as always. A boring sandwich, along with bottled water and some tinned dessert of fruit or pudding, depending on the day. This food and the coffee, made love to my taste buds and after I was finished eating I simply lay down upon the blanket, satiated. I stared up at the bright blue sky, feeling better than I had in years.

Heaven. I felt like I was in Heaven, having had such a delicious meal. It was the first decent meal since I had been shipped off to prison.

I felt sleepy and closed my eyes. It would be just for a few minutes as I was sure I had not used the entire lunch hour. The two men would come when it was their time with me.

I languished in the warmth of the bright autumn sunlight and felt all my aches and pains disintegrate as I drifted off, wrapped in memories of the red-hot sex I'd had with my ex, the man I had accidentally killed. Yeah, he'd been an asshole but he'd been unquenchable in bed. He'd given me plenty of orgasms as long as I reciprocated, and I'd been eager to please.

I wouldn't be so eager to please these two prison guards. I had learned my lesson not to give too much unless I got something in return first. People would have to earn my trust. Not that I could ever trust these two. Especially in the situation I now found myself in.

A strange noise filtered through my drowsiness and I slowly opened my eyes.

Dixon and Ashton stood on each side of me. They were staring down at me with their predatory gazes and my breath halted as I realized both men were completely nude. They possessed big erections. Long and thick cocks.

"Your time is up. Our time has begun," Dixon said in a guttural voice. He was ready to get on with this and so was I, but why were they naked? I hadn't agreed to them actually penetrating me. At least not yet.

I blinked as Dixon held out his hand.

"You need to stand so you can get out of your clothes," he said.

His blue eyes were on fire and I felt the heat moving through me as well.

I noticed he was holding out a key.

"Remove your shoes and socks first and then the ankle restraints. Don't even think about running or tossing away the key. We have an emergency one," Dixon growled.

And here I thought he was holding out his hand because he was going to help me to my feet. Chivalry was indeed dead.

I did as he instructed and removed my shoes and socks while they watched. Then I grabbed the key from him and jammed it into the lock, loving the sound of the click. In a moment, I removed the ankle cuffs and let the chains rattle as I tossed them aside into the tall grass.

I placed the key into one shoe.

A moment later, I stood, trying to ignore the fact that I was actually free of all restraints. I would have made a run for it, but yeah, no shoes. I'd freeze my feet off in the cold dirt. Besides, I was eager to have Dixon and Ashton's mouths upon my flesh and they were putting on a good show, stroking their erections.

They watched as I stepped out of my jumper. Beneath the jumper I wore prison issue track pants and panties. I slid my fingers beneath the waistband of the clothing and slowly, seductively lowered my pants and panties over my hips and then down my legs. I removed my garments and faced the two men.

Their eyes blazed fire as they visually caressed my naked curves. Their erections had thickened and were flushed red with arousal. My pussy grew hot and swollen and I was creaming hot juices, reacting to the stimulating sight.

"Lie down on the blanket, Queen," Dixon instructed.

My heart cracked like a jackhammer as I lay upon the blanket. The wonderful sunshine beat down on my naked body, embracing me with its intense heat.

"No touching us under any circumstances. If you do, the restraints will be placed on you for the rest of the workday. Understood?" Dixon growled.

I nodded and wondered what the big deal was with them not wanting me to touch them. Were they afraid I was going to wrap an arm around their neck and break it? Or maybe they thought I was going to strangle their balls? I grinned inwardly at those thoughts.

"Lift your knees. Spread your legs," Ashton ordered.

His voice sounded hoarse, and the lust flaring in his brown eyes made me tremble. He ripped open a package and pulled out a pink butt plug. It was pretty big and I wondered if it would hurt.

"Have you worn one of these before?" Ashton asked as he held it up.

"Yes, years ago," I admitted.

"Good. This plug comes already sterile and ready to use. I'll put on lots of lube so it will be go in easy enough. I will insert it. Wear it up to a couple of hours at a time. Start slow. You'll get a tube of lube smuggled in with your supper tonight. I'll put these instructions into your pocket. If anyone finds it, say you found it in the orchard. You won't be lying."

A tube of lube with my supper? Wow, he had that good connections?

He reached down and shoved the instructions into my jumper pocket.

"When we think you're ready for anal, we'll make more concessions where work is concerned. Agreed?"

"Yes," I whispered. Heat fused my cheeks and I was eager to continue.

"I'll put the plug in, after..." he said softly.

My breaths were coming faster at his words. I now realized there seriously would be anal penetration sometime down the line and more work concessions. It appeared sex with my prison guards was going to be an ongoing thing, which really thrilled me. Life in prison just got exciting!

Dixon sat down, cross legged on my left side. He slid his hand between his muscular legs and wrapped his fingers around his thick cock. I gasped as his shaft jerked in his hand.

Such fierce power in that gorgeous looking vein riddled rod. I wanted him thrusting into me, but sensed it wasn't going to happen today. The bastards were teasing me in exposing to me their shafts. Showing me what could be mine. Preparing me for what was coming down the line.

The visual stimulation of seeing Dixon cradling his penis, shot wicked want into me. I was so close to telling them that I wanted them to fuck me with their cocks but I held back. I couldn't give into my full needs, not until I had more concessions from them and I needed their trust in me too so I could use them to make my life easier on the inside.

I clenched my hands into the blankets, resisting the urge to touch Dixon's muscular chest. I didn't want to be in restraints for the rest of the day.

I held my breath as Dixon reached out and cupped my breast with his other hand. He held me like he owned me and licked his lips like he was about to devour something magnificent.

A powerful gush of eagerness raged through me as he lowered his head over my breast.

I moaned as Dixon sucked my tender nipple between his hot firm lips. My plump, red nipple was even more sensitive than yesterday due to what they'd done to me, so there was a tiny bite of pain which actually enhanced the pleasure his mouth was creating.

He must have sensed my discomfort, for he sipped leisurely, like I was a precious wine, not forcefully as yesterday.

Then Ashton's shoulders, pushed against my feet as he lowered himself between my spread knees. He was licking his red lips as he stared at my pussy and a wicked need zipped through me as I awaited his next move.

I didn't have to wait long.

He kissed my inner thighs. His hot mouth caressing my flesh, moving slowly until my thighs were trembling and my body was humming. Then hot hands replaced his mouth and he smoothed his palms up and down, igniting shards of heat.

I gasped at the intensity of his ministrations and found myself creaming easily. I moaned as his palms turned into fingers and he softly stroked toward the clenching apex of my thighs. I hadn't been touched by a man down there for over five years and my pussy was aching for male attention.

I cried out as his fingers touched my labia. Moaned as he pulled apart my pussy lips and dipped two fingers into my wet vagina.

Chapter Seven

My body tightened with expectation as he withdrew and then his sopping fingers slid over my tender clitoris in mind-destroying strokes. He took my tender clit between thumb and fore finger and began a gentle rub that had me writhing and crying out as ravaging pleasure suddenly exploded throughout me.

I was a bomb that had been detonated as he cuddled my clit. I twisted within the pleasure that snapped through me in quivering waves. His voracious mouth fused over my pussy and I screamed as his long, hot tongue slid into my vagina like a little cock, prodding and thrusting against my spasming muscles.

Shuddering convulsions destroyed me and I quickly became a bucking tornado as Ashton eagerly sucked my cream into his mouth.

I felt as if I was now just a hot swollen pussy and one turgid nipple as the men lapped, licked, and stroked.

Raging pleasure sunk bone deep, ripping apart my thoughts and every shred of self-control. I was their puppet, and they were my masters as their mouths slammed pleasure into me over and over until my brain was fried and I was screaming within the climaxes that were easily wrung from me.

Deep down in the back of what was left of my mind, I sensed that Ashton had a pussy juice fetish and he would suck and pleasure me for as long as it took for me to keep producing my cream.

Sweet mercy! My two prison guards had turned me into a vessel for their fetishes and now I was lost within the pleasure they created. I knew I would keep bucking and writhing until they deemed this session was over.

Perspiration blossomed over my flesh as they kept sucking on me. No more thoughts were processing. I was just gone, replaced by an insane machine of lust that would just keep producing for them.

Dear heavens, would I go mad from this exquisite torture?

By the time Officers Dixon and Ashton were finished sucking on me, I was panting and keening from the exquisite pleasure. I'd heard both of them come on groans and strangled gasps while they'd mouth pleasured me. They must have been masturbating while my eyes had been closed and I'd been nicely trapped inside their pleasure vortex.

I was spent after their mouths finally left me. I thought it was over, but then I heard the slurp of lube and remembered the butt plug.

"On your hands and knees, Queen. We need to get you outfitted, then we need to get back to work. We need to meet a certain quota," Ashton ordered.

I kind of liked how they'd nicknamed me Queen. There didn't appear to be sarcasm in Ashton's voice as he'd said it, so I hoped they'd gotten the message when I'd told them I was a queen and wanted to be treated better.

I could barely move but I managed to turn over and got onto my fours upon the rumpled blanket. My vagina was raw and open after being sucked so much and my inner thighs were sticky from my cream. My big breasts hung down and I noticed how red and extra plump my one nipple had gotten from Dixon's eager mouth. It felt bruised and used, but nicely so.

"You'll enjoy wearing this plug, I'm sure. Once your ass has becomes accustomed to it, there are bigger sizes," Ashton said from behind me.

"Yes, we want our Queen to be open and juicy for us," Dixon said as he slipped on his underwear. I almost moaned as I watched his limp shaft disappear inside the garment. He was smiling happily as he slipped on his prison issue uniform and was gone.

It appeared he had gotten the satisfaction he'd wanted by sucking my cream out of me.

I hissed as Ashton's lubed finger suddenly pressed against my sphincter. He wasn't wasting any time, was he?

"Just stay loose and relax," he muttered.

Easier said than done when someone was trying to stick a finger into my back door. But I did the best I could and impulsively moaned some more when my tight ring of muscles gave way and he slipped his digit inside.

"I should take you right now. Your pussy cream was so delicious that I came just from the taste of it," he whispered.

"Do you think I'm your slut?" I hissed back at him. I wanted him to take me but I was exhausted, mentally and physically.

I also wanted to remind him I should be treated like a Queen, or at least as best as a prisoner who is giving free sex to her guards should be treated.

"You're not our slut, you are our saviour," he growled.

I stiffened at his confession.

"How so?" I asked.

He said nothing as he withdrew his finger. The slurp of lube followed. I moaned as he pressed two slippery fingers inside my anus.

"You're saving our marriages. Our wives won't cater to our fetishes, so we come to the prison girls, like you."

So, they were married. Disappointment rocked me. They were going behind their wives back. That meant they were not to be trusted. Ever.

"Glad I can be of assistance," I muttered.

He remained silent after that. Perhaps he realized he'd said too much? I gasped as my muscles clenched like a vice around his fingers.

He withdrew. More slurps of lube followed and then something larger than his two fingers pushed against my sphincter. I knew it was the smooth narrow head of the butt plug. I could feel that it had been generously lubed too.

"Just relax," he once again instructed.

I blew out a tense breath and he slowly, cautiously pushed in. It got bigger because of the flared area and then it got narrow again until it was in.

I felt relieved and concentrated on the foreign object buried inside of me. It was an invasion, but I knew from past experience I would get used to it fast.

"Now, we need to get back to work," Ashton instructed. He said nothing more as he hurriedly dressed and then he headed out to the field. To my surprise, Dixon was out there, cutting the stems on the pumpkins.

Huh, now look at that. The ornaments were actually working again. Who would have figured?

I reached for my clothes, feeling the butt plug stretching into my ass with my every movement. Suddenly I wished one of the men was taking me back there. To feel a cock thrusting in and out of my ass would be nice. I remember my asshole ex had enjoyed anal to the point where I'd found myself enjoying it as well.

Heck, I'd take anal over picking pumpkins.

I chuckled to myself and didn't move extra fast in dressing myself. After I had my clothing on, I slipped on my socks and shoes and then I froze.

They'd forgotten to shackle me.

I could run for it.

Good heavens! I should make a run for it!!

I'd just had the most fantastic sex with the two prison guards and now an opportunity to escape had come my way. It should be a no brainer. Run or not to run? The question danced in my head as I watched Dixon and Ashton working in the field. They didn't so much as look my way.

I stood and kept studying them.

Had they left the restraints off on purpose? Were they testing me? If so, and I decided to run, they would surely catch me, especially now with me being exhausted after feeding them with my body. If I took off they would drop me as their sexual host and pick some other prison girl for their pleasures and I wanted to be pleasured by them. At least for now.

Another idea began to form.

I closed my eyes and cursed myself for what I was about to do.

I headed back to the field and joined them. Was I an idiot? Or was I smart for not running?

Dixon and Ashton looked up as I approached but said nothing and quickly returned to the pumpkin work. I pretended not to notice I was restraint free. It was best if they thought I was a docile submissive...well kind of.

Hopefully, this wasn't a one-time occurrence in them forgetting, that is if they forgot. If they had, then yeah, I was an idiot for not taking the opportunity. But if they began to see I wasn't going to run, then I could get their trust and maybe, just maybe, they would leave the restraints off and I would have a better shot at an escape in the future, especially if I could figure out how to get a hold of that prison van.

It was a chance I was willing to take in staying, especially for more of that naughty sex I'd just had.

We worked quietly. We took our breaks separately and at the end of the workday, Dixon produced the restraints and within a minute I was once again in them. But I didn't feel dejected anymore. I had hope now. And some more hot sex on the horizon. No complaints here. Except for the prison food.

As promised a tube of lube was stashed beneath a napkin when my tray with supper was delivered through the slot. I didn't even bother to gaze up at the guard or wave a hello, which I often did when he slid open the Peeping Tom peep hole to check if I had escaped.

In solitary any face was welcome. But tonight, I was just thinking about tomorrow and the sex.

I found myself wondering if I was experiencing the Stockholm Syndrome phenomenon where a captive begins to have feelings for their captor. I didn't know for sure if I were a case, but I did know I would never develop feelings for them.

I would from here on out use them. I would make them comfortable in trusting me. I would study them. Discover their routine where I was concerned and pay particular attention to the vehicles they used, because a vehicle would be essential in my getaway.

And tonight I wouldn't be doing any masturbating. I'd keep myself excited for them. It would make the sexual contact that much more intense tomorrow.

Chapter Eight

I spent the evening as all the other ones, reading, playing Solitaire on my laptop, supper, and so on, but with one change.

In my mind I'd keep a notebook of all possibilities of escape and when the time came and I had a sure-fire chance of getting out of the prison system and fleeing. I would take it.

I mean I had done half my time here already, but anything could happen to keep me here for years beyond my minimum sentence. It wasn't a chance I was willing to take.

In the meantime, I'd enjoy the sexual perks Dixon and Ashton were handing over to me, which made me wonder what they had in store for me tomorrow.

I smiled.

Tomorrow couldn't get here soon enough.

THE NEXT MORNING WAS my access to the shower. We were able to shower three times a week in the shower room. That's another reason I enjoyed solitary. I showered alone, except for the female guard on the other side of the open stall.

After my shower I dressed, had breakfast and was ready to head out.

Promptly I was picked up by one of the guards in charge at solitary. I was escorted to where Dixon and Ashton waited in the garage at the prison van. I noted it was the same vehicle as yesterday. Same licence plate.

I was ushered inside the van, with wrist and leg restraints, and while we drove, the two men remained silent as always.

Ashton drove and I could see he was glancing at me in the rear-view mirror every once in awhile. I don't know why as there was a camera in an upper corner behind him. Unless it wasn't working.

I ignored him and began to take inventory of the interior of the van.

The screened partition between the two guards and me was padlocked and it would prevent me from jumping them. Not that I could overpower two men.

The two exits all had screen doors too and I assumed padlocked on the other side.

There was nothing in here except the uncomfortable metal seats and the windows that allowed me to see that today was a cloudy day outside. It looked dreary and grey. A lot of the colorful leaves had left their trees, leaving most of them barren.

In conclusion of my inspection I could see there was nothing in here that I could use as a weapon in a future escape attempt. But that didn't dismay me. I'd just keep my eyes open for opportunities. Surely there would be better ones than the one I'd had yesterday.

We drove along the same long lone highway as always. Finally I spotted a couple of prison vans that were parked in secluded laneways as we passed. Then came a couple of chain gangs of eight women in each gang who were raking leaves and picking up garbage out of the ditches. I recognized a couple of the women whom I'd travelled with in a prison van on my first day out of the prison.

To think I had narrowly missed being there in the ditch with them. I was quite thrilled I was having sex instead of listening to bitchy cronies and raking all day or picking up garbage.

Moments later we turned onto the same gravel road we'd previously used, but this time we stopped earlier, which made me pray that there were no pumpkins on the other side of this row of evergreen trees.

I'd grown sick of picking pumpkins. My arms, thighs and back were sore from all that bending and lifting. But I wasn't sick of the sex. I needed to be pleasured today, especially because I hadn't taken the edge off last night.

"Alright, Queen. Time to work," Dixon said as he slid open the side door and that's when I realized there was no padlock on that metal barred screen as he slid it open. Why had I never noticed that before?

Excitement rushed through me as I jumped out of the van.

Had the padlock always been missing?

Man, becoming observant certainly did raise opportunities of escape.

"Still wearing your plug?" Ashton asked as he and Dixon ushered me through the row of dense pine trees.

"Yes, as you instructed. I'm taking care of it. No worries," I replied brightly. I wanted him to think I was being submissive.

Inside I chuckled. But my chuckling stalled when I spied what we'd be doing today.

"Apple trees?" I questioned as I stared along the rows and rows of trees heavily laden with bright red apples. My mouth watered as I imagined biting into one.

"You'll be picking and we'll be dumping and sorting," Dixon answered.

"Can we eat them?" I asked, suddenly realizing I had fresh fruit.

"As many as you want, " he said.

Wow! Cool! This was good. I loved apples and it was rare to get a nice red one in prison. Having them fresh off a tree was something I'd never experienced before.

Dixon proceeded to hand me a lightweight yellow plastic basket with a handle. There was a hook dangling off the handle.

"Hang the basket by hooking the hook on the nearby branches as you pick. You'll start picking around the bottom of the trees. Handle the apples like eggs. Then you grab a ladder and start your way up.

Bring the full baskets to us at the bin." He pointed to several aluminum twenty-foot ladders that had been leaned against a nearby tree and then to the row of wood slat bins that were laid out down the rows of apple trees.

"Hold out your hands," Dixon said in a cool command. His blue eyes seemed icy cold in the grey ambiance of our surroundings.

I did as I was told, feeling excitement shift through me as he uncuffed my wrists and then he let the chains drop into the grass.

"Undo her leg restraints," he ordered Ashton, who stood nearby.

The cool autumn wind was blowing from behind Ashton and I caught a gentle whiff of soap. He smelled good. I liked a clean man who smelled good, especially when I was going to have sex with him.

Ashton nodded and did as he was told. I would have had a clear shot at the back of his neck if I'd had a weapon, but I noticed Dixon had placed his hand on the handle of his gun.

Okay, he didn't trust me. Yet.

"And what did you want in return today for allowing me to go without restraints?" I asked.

"You'll be wearing an ankle monitor instead of restraints. You'll be able to climb the ladder easier."

My hopes plummeted at the mention of the ankle monitor.

Damn! I should have known. No escape today.

"We'll discuss a proposition for you at first break," Ashton said as he quickly put on the ankle monitor.

And just like that, my hopes were high again.

No escape today, but definitely some red-hot sex!

I could hardly wait for break-time to find out what they had in store for me!

The job went easy enough and when break time came, I was eager to find out what the two prison guards would propose they wanted to do sexually to me. If I played my cards right, in return for my submission, they'd be doing my job hauling the heavy baskets of apples to the bin and I would be doing their job of dumping and sorting.

At break, I received my traditional tall paper cup filled with ice-cold water and then a second helping. They'd also supplied a nice, folded blanket for me to sit on while I stared off into the distance at the tall yellowing grass beneath the apple-laden trees we still had to work on. I figured we'd be here for at least a few more days. The area was secluded, just like the pumpkin patch had been.

I'd munched on several apples while working in the trees or up the ladder. The fruit was juicy and so delicious and sweet that I wondered how I could smuggle a couple of apples back into the prison with me. I doubted I could get one inside because every time I returned from being outdoors, I was physically patted down and a metal detector waved all around my body parts.

I was crunching on yet another sweet apple as I sat waiting for them to make their proposition for today.

Finally, they approached and towered over me while I continued to sit. The air was getting warmer now, and thankfully the sun was peeking out from between the clouds splashing sunshine here and there.

"We have a proposition for you, for after lunch," Dixon said. His eyes weren't as icy cold now that the weather was improving which for some crazy reason made me feel better.

"Okay, shoot," I said after swallowing a bite.

"Yesterday you had the pleasure of oral from me," Ashton said. "I'd like you to return the favor on me."

I inhaled at that idea. I'd done oral to my late ex many times so I knew what to do.

I turned to look up at Dixon.

"And you?"

"I'll be taking him anally while you do him orally."

Oh. Okay. This was different. However there was just one problem.

"What pleasures do I get out of the deal?" I requested directly.

"What did you want?" Dixon asked.

Wow, a wide-open possibility. The thought about forgoing being pleasured today and simply getting them to work for me the rest of the day shot through my mind. However, I knew I'd be bored with that request. I wanted more.

"Do you have condoms?" I asked.

I noticed both men stiffen.

Chapter Nine

"We do," Ashton replied coolly. He reached into his breast pocket and produced several packets of condoms. He fanned them on the blanket beside me.

"Then I want some red-hot vaginal sex and I want to be able to touch you with one of you taking me while both of you are kissing me. I want to be pleasured like the Queen that I am."

Ashton and Dixon looked at each other with what I could only interpret as an endearing look. Understanding suddenly whipped through me. These two men must be gay or more likely bisexual. Maybe in love with each other? Yesterday Ashton had said I was their savior. That their wives didn't want to do things with them and that was why they came to the prisoners.

"All this is going to cut into the work time," Dixon suddenly said.

Well, if he thought I was going to give up breaks and lunch, he could forget it. However he was neatly falling into my plan.

"Then I suggest you two do the picking and dumping of the apples into the bins and I do the sorting. Two men work much faster than one woman. Deal?"

I held my breath as I awaited their answer.

"Deal," Ashton said. "But after lunch, we go first and then you get pleasured."

Hmm I preferred to have my payment up front, however I realized I was getting a good deal with them doing my job anyways, so why push my luck.

"Deal."

"We start after lunch. Break time is up. Ashton and I will start with the picking now, then we won't have to rush this afternoon," Dixon said. He nodded to his partner and they both headed back to the orchard.

I couldn't stop myself from smiling.

Man, life was getting so much better having these two men around. I would have an easy day of work, do some oral and then get pleasured. Why would I want to escape from that?

I hid my smiles as I headed back to work.

Lunch came quickly and to my surprise, Dixon shared his home-made meal with me. He didn't say anything as he handed me a droolworthy half a foot long submarine sandwich drenched with bacon, tomato, mayo, pickles and lettuce. Ashton gave me a bag of potato chips along with a soft drink can. In prison, we weren't allowed cans for fear we'd use them as missiles when throwing them at someone or makeshift shanks made out of the metal to slice or stab someone.

So, having a can in my hand, was bliss. It also meant trust was forming with them towards me. And that in my book was a good thing.

They strolled down a ways and ate by themselves, speaking in hushed tones like lovers would do. The way they smiled at each other made me think that yeah, something was going on between them. But it wasn't my business. I just wanted some pleasure and an easy workday.

Eagerness barrelled through me, as a little while later, Dixon gazed at his watch. He said something to Ashton, who looked my way and then he nodded.

I'd finished lunch a long time ago and had been trying hard not to let what was about to happen get in the way of me relaxing in the sunshine. But it did get in the way and I couldn't wait to touch them because I hadn't touched a man in so long that it was insane.

I gazed down at the condoms that had been placed on the blankets and shivered as my pussy clenched with an intense need for penetration. I would be getting some good old-fashioned sex after I gave the men what they wanted.

I held my breath as I saw the two prison guards approaching.

Show time.

Ashton and Dixon removed their weapon laden utility belts and placed them upon some nearby bushes. Then they detached their radios and took off their shoes. Their uniforms came next as I watched them.

I was feeling pretty flushed as their muscle-toned bodies emerged. They were in really good shape. I had noticed it yesterday but too many naughty things were happening to me for me to fully comprehend and appreciate these men's bodies.

Just thinking about what they wanted me to do to Ashton had me energized. The two prison guards had fetishes, yet they were also gay, but more likely bisexual as they'd gotten aroused seeing me naked.

Maybe they were closet bisexuals? Whatever they were, I needed to remind myself that their sexual orientation really was none of my business.

They looked dominant and dangerous, their eyes full of lust as they gazed at each other and continued to undress. Power oozed off their hard bodies in heated waves. They were two men on a mission as their cocks unfurled from the restraints of their underwear. They were both fully erect. Aroused and engorged. They were exceptionally well hung and their long thick shafts were ready for action.

My heart began to pound as they dropped their garments onto a heap beside the blanket.

"Get undressed," Dixon growled at me. "We want you naked."

I nodded meekly and did their bidding, placing my clothing beside theirs, keeping note of how easy it would be right at this moment for me to slip a gun out of one of their holsters and point it at them. Maybe shoot them dead and make a getaway.

But I wasn't ready yet. I needed more details. Like did they check in with the prison during the day? What times? Where did they keep the keys to the prison van? How would I be able to escape without being noticed when I was in that van? Where would I go when I made a run for it?

Too many things to think about and a bunch of problems to solve. When I made my escape, I wanted it to go smoothly. There would be more opportunities soon. I would have to wait until I had a vivid plan, preparing for all contingencies.

I had a butt plug up my ass. That was my insurance that they would be keeping me around for a little while anyways. In the meantime, I could get more enjoyment out of these two.

My breaths came faster and I swallowed, then I nervously licked my lips, preparing myself for Ashton. I hadn't done oral on a man in years, but it was kind of like riding a bicycle, you never forgot how to do it.

Ashton came and stood in front of me.

"On your knees, and sit up straight, Queen," he ordered.

I did as instructed and got on my knees, sitting straight so that my breasts poked out at him.

"Don't try anything funny. No strangling my balls or biting my cock off or you'll disappear without a trace. Is that clear?" Ashton said.

His voice was cold and I knew he was serious. I suddenly realized I had to be very careful with his sensitive part. I also grasped that there was a good chance that they would do away with me anyways once they fulfilled their future fantasies. I would be a loose end if I decided to talk and they would be in deep shit if someone in the prison system believed me.

Dread dropped over me like a cold blanket and my innocence was gone. I got the creepy feeling my days might be numbered. That plan I was devising would have to come sooner rather than later if I were to survive these two prison guards.

I nodded and forced myself not to think about what might happen in the future. Right now I was safe and I would enjoy myself.

Man, maybe I was a Stockholm Syndrome case after all?

"You know what to do," Ashton said as he gazed down at me.

I reached out and gingerly curled one hand around the base of his thick shaft. His flesh felt hot and it jerked as I started stroking up and down his length. His penis grew even bigger and bigger and he began moaning.

His gaze was intense as he reached out. His long fingers slid through my hair at the sides of my head. He gripped me hard, holding my head steady and then he moved his hips forward.

His cockhead was a mere inch from my face and I opened my mouth, suddenly eager to please. Hell, I'd better please or I *would* mysteriously disappear.

Behind him, I heard Dixon ripping open a condom package. Moments later, the heavy slurps of lube followed. My vaginal muscles clenched at the erotic sounds. Soon it would be my turn, but first Ashton needed his pleasure.

Pulsing hot lust shot through me as he pushed his feverish cockhead into my mouth.

Ashton's shaft stretched and burned my quaking lips and I wasted no time in moving my head forward, allowing him to slide in further. I stopped when he touched the back of my throat.

Then I moved my head back about an inch and wrapped my other hand around his cock right outside my mouth so when he withdrew and began to thrust, my hand would prevent his penis from going all the way into my throat and making me gag.

I gave him a nod and Ashton began a slow drive, in and out, and I tightened my lips around his penis, giving him a good pressure. Suddenly there came a bit of a buck and Ashton's cock slid deeper and I heard him gasp.

That meant Dixon had to be penetrating him anally now. I looked up at Ashton's face and saw his mouth hanging open and his eyes scrunched tight. His pistoning became faster and I hollowed out my cheeks giving him more compression.

He moaned and gasped again. He liked what Dixon and I were doing to him.

Ashton's cock filled my mouth and then he withdrew. Then Dixon penetrated him again, pushing Ashton's shaft back into my mouth. Over and over we went. We got into an arousing rhythm and before long both men were moaning and groaning.

Whimpers escaped my mouth as I grew excited and needy imagining both of these prison guards eventually thrusting into me. My nipples elongated, my ass clenched around the plug and my pussy juices began to seep out of me.

My mouth was seared with heat and my lips felt bruised as Ashton continued plunging in and out. His cock thickened and jerked in my mouth and his breaths grew faster and faster. His thrusts grew harder and harder.

Chapter Ten

"**I**'m coming!" Ashton suddenly cried out.

A few more solid thrusts and then hot jets of his release flooded my mouth. Quickly I swallowed and kept sucking and sucking on his hot spasming flesh until he was dry.

Then he removed his cock from my mouth and Dixon withdrew from Ashton, who then wearily sat down at the edge of the blanket beside me. His breathing was harsh and his eyes were dark with excitement.

"That was so good," Ashton complimented.

"Glad to be of service," Dixon replied, his eyes twinkling with happiness as he carefully removed the condom from his very erect cock. I could tell that Dixon liked that Ashton had experienced a good release.

"Take her," he breathed, nodding to Dixon's big erection.

Dixon grinned and leaned over his clothing to pick up a small packet of wet wipes. Quickly he cleaned his hands with one and tossed the package to me.

Goodness, these men came prepared. I wiped my hands and whimpered as Dixon grabbed a new condom and quickly sheathed it onto his engorged penis.

His blue eyes glimmered like jewels as he held out his hand to me.

"Stand, Queen," he ordered in a guttural tone.

Huh, I guess chivalry wasn't dead after all.

I placed my palm against his and he easily hoisted me to my feet. Then he let go and his hands slid upon my hips like two scorching brands of possession.

"You can touch me as per our agreement. Ashton will do the same to you," Dixon whispered in a rasping tone.

Ashton was back on his feet and had stepped behind me. His body heat whipped against my back, warming me and I shuddered as his hot hands cupped my ass cheeks. He leaned against me and began fanning feather light kisses across the back of my shoulders. It felt so good to finally be touched by a man again and I moaned my thanks.

Dixon's warm breath caressed my face and I trembled as he closed his eyes and lowered his head. His hot mouth slammed over mine in a fierce ownership that had my head spinning. His tongue forced itself between my lips and stroked my teeth and gums, making me heady.

I grabbed his waist, relishing the tautness of his body and held on for dear life as my world tilted. I'd never been kissed so forcefully before, and I felt like a virgin in unfamiliar territory. Sparkles of pleasure snapped through my nipples as he buffed his hot muscular chest all over my breasts.

He squished his cockhead against my engorged clitoris and began rubbing and grinding me there. My lower body tightened, my inner thighs quivered and my pussy felt hot, swollen and dripped with my juices.

I sensed I could come at any minute.

Dixon nipped and suckled at my lips with his kisses, leaving dainty little stings behind as he continued all the way around my mouth. By the time he was finished my upper and lower lips were on fire.

Then his mouth melted over mine again and I felt possessed. He slid his cockhead off my quivering clit and plunged an inch into my wet vagina. His silk-encased flesh throbbed teasingly there.

"Touch me," he whispered as he broke the kiss.

I barely heard him through the buzzing in my ears and the panting of my breath.

I smoothed my hands between our bodies, fanning my palms over his hot chest muscles, feeling them jerk beneath my fingers. I found a nipple and pinched it gently, then rubbed and caressed it until it became rock hard and he was moaning. I did the same to his other nipple until his breaths came hard and fast.

Ashton's hands were smoothing seductively up and down my arms and he was pressing himself against my butt plug. Insistently, but not too hard. The plug felt like a cock buried deep inside my ass. The pressure was intense and bruisingly beautiful.

Was this how it was going to feel when they both finally took me?

I couldn't wait to find out how a threesome with double penetration would unfold, but right now Dixon and Ashton were doing a magnificent job in pleasuring me.

Ashton's kisses intensified. His hot lips danced over the back of my neck making me shiver. The intoxicating way he pushed against my behind making that butt plug move inside my ass had me moaning.

Dixon's mouth was fused over mine, sliding back and forth as his cock worked deeper and deeper into my sopping vagina with every penetration. He was going agonizingly slow because of the tightness created by the plug and I was at the edge of having an orgasm.

I just needed a little extra stimulation.

As if finally sensing what I craved, Dixon withdrew and forcefully drove his cock into me all the way. I shuddered as every thick inch of his solid penis stretched into my ultra-tight vagina.

He pulled out and began a driving thrust. The added friction was exactly what I needed. Spasms exploded throughout and I went wild as an orgasm rocked through me. Shudders embraced me and I bucked and gyrated between the two men.

Dixon was pumping so wickedly and Ashton was moving that butt plug so nicely that I got lost inside the brutal firestorm raging in me.

It was agony, bliss and pleasure, all rolled into one. I was gasping, moaning and keening as my vaginal muscles tightened and quivered and pulsed around Dixon's intrusion and my ass clenched the plug.

Dixon pistoned faster and faster and then he ripped his mouth from mine. He cried out his pleasure as he came.

Somewhere in the back of my mind I knew it the instant it happened. The second his hot release flooded my insides; I knew the condom had broken.

Oh shit.

But I was so wrapped inside my own climax I just couldn't stop my vagina from milking his seed. Couldn't stop gyrating or keening or stopping myself as I flew into a red-hot second orgasm. It rocked me harder than the first one, and both men carried me through it. Their kisses, their heated touches swept over my quivering hot flesh. They knew where to caress me, knew how to keep my pussy milking Dixon for so long that I would have gone on forever, it was so beautiful.

The rush of convulsions was spectacular. Like nothing I had ever experienced before.

Pleasure ravaged me as I mindlessly convulsed between the bodies of the two prison guards. Finally the climax ebbed away and I was physically spent.

Dixon withdrew and surely enough his condom had ripped. He bit his bottom lip, a sheepish smile on his face as he held up the condom for us to see.

"Looks like your pregnancy woman fetish might be coming true after all," Ashton said and elbowed Dixon, who winked at me.

Son of a bitch.

If I didn't know any better, I would think he'd sabotaged that condom in the first place.

My heart was pounding at an insane pace as I plopped down onto the blanket, feeling both dejected and elated, if that was possible.

I could be pregnant. If I were, there really wasn't anything I could do about it anyway, so why fret?

Dixon and Ashton sat down on the blanket with me, then the two men lay down on their sides, facing each other. Dixon ordered me to spoon against his backside, which I obediently did.

A few minutes later, both prison guards were snoring softly.

But I remained wide awake. What if I was pregnant? If I stayed in the prison system Dixon and Ashton might decide to keep me around just because of Dixon's pregnancy fetish. Or they might want to get rid of me because the DNA in the baby would prove we'd had sex.

I had a big decision to make, didn't I? Especially now that I could be thinking for two instead of just me.

To escape and live on the run with a baby or stay in the prison on work detail and take my chances that Dixon and Ashton wouldn't make me disappear.

Things just got seriously complicated.

I had a lot to think about.

The rest of the day went by uneventfully as we worked beneath the gorgeous autumn sunshine.

I'd been watching the guards as they worked and it appeared as if they were not in any regular communication with the prison. They wore their weapons at all times, except for when we had sex. I'd also discovered where they kept the keys to the van.

Whomever drove, put the key into their breast pocket along with the keys to my chains, which I continued to wear before the work began and at the end of the day after we were finished working and before I was ushered back to the van.

A plan of escape was formulating now as the workday drew to a close. A few more days of this routine and more observations, I sensed I might be ready to make my escape attempt.

Back at the prison, in isolation, I opted not to masturbate after lights out, realizing I got more sexual satisfaction from the prison guards.

Pondering that Dixon might have made me pregnant had me seesawing between giddiness and disappointment. Having a baby in prison would be a no no for me. They wouldn't let me keep it, and who would take it? There was no way I would give a kid of mine up for adoption, nor would I abort. The only person I could think of who might stand by me and take my baby was my sister who I hadn't heard from since I'd come in here.

Heck, I didn't even know where she lived.

Having a baby on the run, if I did manage to escape, would be the better option.

The next few days went the same way as the last few. There was no mention of the possibility of my being pregnant but the sex continued to be scorching hot. Ashton inserted a larger butt plug one afternoon and that night a new tube of lube had been delivered with my supper tray just like the last time.

Chapter Eleven

Every new day we agreed on what would happen during sex. I got work concessions and I really did feel like a Queen. The prison guards brought me home-made lunches and I loved all the food. Drench worthy roast beef sandwiches, mouth-watering salmon sandwiches, fresh garden salads, and even cold steak burgers.

My guards were growing careless during and after sex, to the point we were all beginning to take naps after our sessions, spooned against each other on a blanket they always supplied.

Yup, this was as good as freedom. Almost.

Another thing I noticed. I was becoming addicted to sex with my prison guards. I couldn't wait to get to work. Couldn't wait to have sex and at times my plans for freedom would wane.

However, I kept reminding myself that they could and probably would make me mysteriously disappear when they tired of me. It wouldn't be hard either. Kill me, bury me and just say I had escaped.

So, yeah, my addiction to their hot sex would have to take a back seat to my addiction to wanting to live.

One morning, I noticed something was different about Dixon and Ashton as Ashton drove us to the apple orchard in the prison van. The two men were quieter than usual. Their bodies tense. Their gazes toward me lustier.

Something naughty was in the air and instinctively I knew today was the day when both of them would take me at the same time.

My pussy quivered and my ass clenched at the idea. I'd never been double penetrated before. Not by flesh and blood, well-hung men. I grew hot just thinking about it.

As I stepped out of the prison van, Dixon and Ashton, swooped in around me. Their eyes were bright with eagerness and their cocks impressively tented their pants. They were already aroused and so was I. My nipples felt bigger than usual, my pussy hung heavy and hot with need and my anal muscles were jerking around the plug with anticipation.

If I had my way, I'd have told them to take me right then and there, but I had other plans also circulating in my head for today.

"Today is the day," Dixon said, his blue eyes piercing me and making me tremble.

"We'll start right after lunch," Ashton replied in a giddy voice.

"Remove your plug during first break and then you'll be ready for both of us. We'll take you after lunch," Dixon instructed.

I nodded jerkily. My legs were jittery as I followed them to the apple orchard.

They removed my wrist and ankle chains and then Ashton placed the ankle monitor, reminding me that if I tried to take it off, or if I went more than a mile in any direction from them, the alarm would alert them as well as alert the prison.

Over the last few days, I'd discovered that Ashton used special tools to tighten the strap around the ankle bracelet and that he pushed a button on the little black box attached after securing it and before removing it. He kept the small tools that would remove the restraint in his breast pocket with the other keys.

I inhaled deeply as I gazed around the orchard and waited for Dixon and Ashton to bring me the first baskets full of apples so I could dump and sort them in the bin. Yup, there was still more work to be done. Still plenty of apples on the trees to be picked.

But today was *the* day.

Today, everything would come to a head.

Since deciding I would make an escape attempt I'd observed my two prison guards like my life depended on it. They were predictable and that would hopefully be their downfall and make my escape successful. Having a ménage before clearing out would be the icing on the cake, so to speak. It would be something to remember them by, just as a potential baby would be.

I smiled and resisted the urge to touch my abdomen. This baby, that is if I were pregnant, would be wanted by me even with it being an accident.

AT FIRST BREAK, THE men were exuberant in outlining what they planned to do to me after lunch and I had to admit I was seriously aroused and excited for them to take me. They agreed to work concessions and I behaved as if nothing was different. I knew that if I failed to escape, years would be added to my sentence, but if I didn't escape, I might be dead.

I really had no choice, did I?

Lunch couldn't come soon enough and when they presented me with a huge Chicken Caesar Salad sandwich, my mouth exploded with gratitude as I devoured the wonderful food.

I couldn't help but moan and groan my appreciation as the tangy flavors exploded against my tongue and made love to my taste buds. I noticed the two men would tense every time I made my noises, even though they sat twenty feet away eating and talking to each other in hushed tones.

Yup, they were definitely bisexual. Of that I had no doubt.

I also had no doubts that I would miss the sex.

My heart skipped a beat when lunch time was over and Dixon and Ashton walked over to me.

"Did you remove the plug as instructed?" Ashton asked.

"Yes, during break," I replied.

I don't know why he was asking as they'd watched me disappear during break after we'd worked out concessions. I'd walked a couple of rows over and done the deed, dropping the plug in a clump of tall grass beneath one of the apple trees that had already been picked clean. At this point I didn't care if the farmer or his helpers found it. Didn't care that it was unhygienic. Not my problem.

The only things on my mind had been my escape and the hot sex I'd be getting.

The two prison guards had done most of the work this morning, leaving me refreshed and ready to participate in a naughty little send off before I left for good.

The time had finally come for both.

"Get naked," Dixon instructed.

"You two get naked first. I want to watch a nice strip tease," I smiled inwardly at the surprise bursting in their eyes. Until now I'd been submissive during sex. Today, I'd trade things up.

"Okay," Ashton said slowly, a little amused smirk on his lips. He reached for his utility belt with weapons attached and unlatched it.

"You are the Queen," Dixon said and to my amusement, he bowed to me.

For a split second I had the intense feeling that these two men would never hurt or kill me. I clamped down on that unexpected feeling and concentrated on watching them.

Dixon removed his belt.

Excitement pulsed through me as they casually dropped their belts into the nearby tall grass. Their weapons would be easy to reach when the time came.

I licked my tongue teasingly along my lower lip, as I studied them. I made sure to smile and to lower my lashes prettily. May as well go out with a bang.

"Go on," I prodded.

They removed their radios, slowly placing them down on top of their belts.

I noted Ashton remove a tube of lube from his pant pocket. He tossed it onto the blanket near my feet.

"Nice, keep going," I encouraged.

My body was tightening with awareness as both men began to unzip their jackets. The jackets were placed upon their utility belts. Their shirts followed, revealing nicely toned muscles on the prison guards.

My breathing began to quicken as their hands slipped to the zippers on their pants. It was so cool how they both moved in unison, unzipping at the same speed as well-trained strippers. A moment later they both stepped out of their pants and tossed them onto the other clothing.

It didn't go unnoticed by me that they were piling everything upon their weapons, which would make it a bit lengthier to get at what I would need. My attention flew to their rock-hard looking erections pushing boldly against their underwear. I trembled at the sight. It would be in just a few short minutes before both of them took me.

Before they could lower their underwear, I stepped forward, reaching out my hands. I placed a palm on Dixon's hard hot chest and my other palm on Ashton's strong chest. Both men inhaled as I smoothed my hands over their curvy muscles. I found a nipple on each man and gently squeezed and pinched. Their buds beaded and grew hard.

They groaned their approval.

Then I lowered my head and sucked Ashton's hot nipple into my mouth. I suckled him. His hand came up and he grabbed hold of my upper arm and simply held on, panting as I tenderly bit his rigid flesh.

Then I moved over to Dixon's chest, sucking his beaded nipple into my mouth. He swore softly and reached up to cup my clothed breast. The heat from his hand torched me and he quickly found my nipple and began to squeeze and pinch until I was gasping. Ashton did the same, finding my nipple through the layers of clothing, pinching it and rubbing.

Before long I was moaning with pleasure as we all played with each other's nipples.

Man, I'd never done something so erotic before. It was crazy nice playing with men's nipples while they played with mine.

Soon, their hands were leaving my breasts and they began to undress me.

Tension grew inside me as Dixon unzipped my jumper.

The dominant expression on his face made me feel meek. His blue eyes looked stormy hot and my breaths came heavy and fast. I could feel my nipples swelling, and my breasts pushing hard against my top as the jumper was lowered to my waist. Dixon slid his hands under the hem of my top and then lifted. I raised my arms and he slipped my top over my head. He tossed the garment onto the pile of their clothes.

Cool autumn air breathed against my flesh, sending a chill into me. I shivered.

"Easy, we'll get you warm really fast," Ashton whispered from behind me.

He unclipped my bra at the back and it fell away, freeing my big breasts, baring them to Dixon. Appreciation made him smile. Instinctively I knew it was a genuine smile, something that came from deep within a part of him that valued big breasts. The tip of his tongue peeked out from between his lips, making me shiver with want.

"Steady yourself," Dixon instructed.

I grabbed his waist and held tight to him.

Dixon wasted no time. He cupped my breasts with his strong hands, warming me instantly. He lowered his head and his lips gingerly swept over mine in an intoxicating tease that had me whimpering at the onslaught of pleasurable tingles zipping around my mouth. My abdomen clenched as those naughty tingles arrowed down south, hitting my pussy with a big bang and making me cream hot juices.

Need slammed through me as Ashton stepped closer behind. His body heat warmed my backside and he pulled the jumper past my hips and then down my legs. I slid off my shoes and the jumper followed. Then Ashton's fingers dipped beneath the waistband of my pants and panties and he slid my clothing downward.

Despite feeling heady from Dixon's hot kisses, I managed to lift one leg and then the other so Ashton could get rid of the rest of my clothes.

By now I knew Dixon had a breast fetish and that Ashton had an ass fetish. I'd been told that Ashton would take me in the ass. So, it came as no surprise when the slurps of lube lashed through the air. Then his lubed finger caressed against my sphincter until I gave him access.

"She's nicely open back here. The plugs are worth their weight in gold," Ashton muttered.

Dixon didn't respond.

I inhaled sharply as Ashton began to press lube inside and against my eager anal muscles.

I could feel Dixon's big, clothed erection pushing against my lower abdomen. His flesh was a hot knot and his kisses burned my senses.

Chapter Twelve

Having both men touching me like this was whipping a whirlwind of anticipation through me.

Man, I wish I could stay here and get this wicked hot treatment from them every day.

My thoughts disintegrated as Dixon's fingers found my nipples and I moaned into his mouth as he brushed his thumbs over the sensitive tips in an agonizingly slow seduction. His kiss deepened and I bucked beneath the ravaging need inside my pussy as Dixon rubbed his package against me.

The rip of foil from behind had me tensing.

Condom time. Slurps of lube followed and I knew Ashton was lubing his shaft.

I tightened my grip on Dixon and moments later Ashton pushed his condom-sheathed engorged cockhead against my sphincter. I held my breath as he forced his cock deeper, penetrating and pushing his swollen shaft against my tender tissues.

The heat from his flesh was intense. The pressure of his impalement was incredibly beautiful bringing along a bite of pain. I'd never experienced something like this before. So hot in the ass. So big and all consuming. It was like I was being possessed.

Ashton withdrew and I moaned the loss into Dixon's mouth.

Dixon pressed his erection against my clitoris and I gasped as he gyrated there creating intense sensations that was quickly building toward an orgasm. He ripped his mouth away and began a bombardment of intoxicating kisses along my chin and then down the length of my neck, and across my chest.

I felt defenseless as Ashton held tight to my waist and plunged his cock into me again. I cried out at the impact. He withdrew and began a stroking rhythm that had me panting with his every hard thrust. There were so many incredible sensations smothering me. So much pleasure and bits of pain that destroyed my thoughts. I was trapped between their bodies. Lost and defenseless, but so enraptured.

Dixon's mouth captured my quivering nipple and more pleasure sang through me as he nipped and nibbled, licked and lapped. He backed off grinding against my clit and I could only sob with the sensations as Dixon's mouth made love to my nipples and Ashton pistoned his penis into my ass like he was a man possessed.

Dixon tore his mouth away from my nipple and uncupped my breasts. I let go of him and watched as his fingers glided beneath the waistband of his underwear. Then he slid them down over his hips and his cock sprang free, elongating and thickening like a giant snake.

Mercy, but his generous size always enthralled me.

His big cock bobbed as he stepped out of his underwear. Then he moved back in front of me, settling his palms upon my hips. I slapped my hands over his broad shoulders, loving the flexing of his muscles beneath my palms.

His expression was tight with exhilaration. His eyes flashed with heat and his face was flushed red.

"Your nipples are the best I've ever tasted," he complimented.

I couldn't even answer as Ashton pistoned into me again. I bucked and dug my fingernails into Dixon's shoulders, preventing myself from falling. Ashton pulled out and then thrust into me again, his cock strong and solid as my snug anus stretched around him in welcome. Then he withdrew.

Dixon quickly moved closer.

"Get ready for us, Queen," he whispered in a dark guttural voice that dazed my senses.

I moaned as in one wicked thrust Dixon had me impaled on his thick long penis. Somewhere deep in the back of my mind, something warned me to stop.

But I didn't pay attention.

I was already too hot, not wanting to break this mood. Besides all my self-control was gone as both men began an overwhelming thrusting.

In one went. Then out. In the other one went and then out.

The friction of two cocks seared my two intimate openings and I cried out at the bites of intoxicating pain and the shards of blissful pleasure. My thighs and lower belly tightened. My breaths came faster and faster.

I clamped my mouth over Dixon's mouth and thrust my tongue between his lips. He groaned as our tongues mated.

I moaned as their pistoning grew deeper and harder, their powerful bodies sandwiching me between them. Perspiration blossomed over my heated skin and slaps of their flesh pummelling me split through the air.

It didn't take long for me to come because of the earlier erotic stimulation upon my clitoris and nipples, and when I came, I came hard.

Pleasure shot through me like a scorching rocket. I went instinctual, bucking against Ashton, grinding against Dixon, and moaning into the tidal waves of pleasure.

The two prison guards gave me no mercy as they continued spearing their shafts into me. Over and over.

Sharp, hot convulsions pounded me. I twisted between the two men, moaning and whimpering as the exquisite pleasure made love to me. Their driving, profound strokes had me screaming and trembling as their solid heat filled me like I'd never been filled before.

It was so good. Too good.

My body throbbed. My pussy and ass clenched like vice grips around each impalement.

Dixon and Ashton just kept pistoning like a well-oiled machines. Never ending. Continuous.

And so were my orgasms.

I fought for breath as the climaxes consumed me. The pleasures shattered me, drowned me and carried me away to some faraway land where life *was* a climax. A world of pleasure and nothing else.

Sometime later, as I was slowly coming down from yet another wild orgasm, I heard Dixon and Ashton shout out their own releases. Felt heat from condom-captured sperm buried deep inside my ass from Ashton's cock. Jets of semen spurt within my vagina from Dixon. I suddenly realized why my mind had warned me to stop near the beginning.

Dixon hadn't been wearing a condom.

But it was too late anyway. So I just let my pussy milk him of his seed as I shuddered and convulsed and accepted what had happened yet again.

But it didn't really matter. I was pregnant anyway. My period hadn't come and I was always on schedule just like clockwork. Dixon had already put a baby in me.

Afterwards, no one spoke as we all lay down on the blanket, spent.

The warm autumn sunshine warmed our naked bodies and before long Ashton and Dixon were snoring with satisfied smiles on their faces.

Unfortunately, I had no time for languishing.

When I heard their breathing deepen and slow, I moved quickly yet quietly off the blanket. Gingerly I dressed in Ashton's prison guard uniform and slipped on his hat.

Then I buckled Ashton's heavy weapon laden belt around my waist. I grabbed Dixon's belt and both of the radios.

Holding my breath as fear pummelled me, I threw quick glances at the two sleeping prison guards and unbuttoned Ashton's shirt pocket. I located the two little tools that Ashton used to open and close my ankle monitor.

In a moment, the monitor dropped off my ankle and I pushed the button just like I'd seen Ashton do. I tossed the monitor off into the trees and then slipped my hand into the other breast pocket.

Shivers of both dread and excitement shot through me as I curled my fingers around the key to the van. I left the key there. For now.

I felt lightheaded with terror, despite being armed now, as I moved with the radios and weapons down the main row of apple trees to where we'd first started working this morning.

I dropped the items and picked up my ankle chains where they'd been left after Ashton had outfitted me with the ankle monitor. I left the wrist restraints and weapons there.

Despite my holding the ankle restraints gently and carefully in my hands, they still tinkled slightly. The noise zapped through the air like an explosion.

I froze. Had the guards heard?

I gazed down to where they lay on the blanket. Neither naked man moved.

My heart was beating so hard it felt like it was going to go through my chest as I began to move again and approached them.

I had to be crazy to be risking myself in hanging around here and doing what I was about to do to them, but I needed extra time to get away. I moved to their feet and crouched down.

I slid an open restraint under one of Dixon's ankles and clicked it shut, then with the other end, I cuffed Ashton's ankle. The two men were now cuffed naked to each other.

They continued to sleep.

Man, how lucky could I be?

I gave them one long last look as doubt crept into my mind. Should I leave or should I stay? No, I had to make a run for it. I'd be stupid to at least not try.

The sex had been good, but it was over.

Despite my wanting to run like a woman possessed, I tiptoed quietly once again back to where we'd started working this morning.

I gazed back. They continued to sleep.

For a brief moment regret flowed through me. They'd trusted me. Had figured I was too submissive to make a run for it.

They'd been wrong.

I shook away the regret, grabbed Dixon's weapon belt and the radios and slipped into the treeline.

Moments later I was at the van.

Exhilaration and an insane need to move fast raged through me. But despite my anxiety, I quietly opened the door and climbed into the driver's seat. I tossed the items onto the passenger seat, then slammed the key into the ignition and turned.

The engine rumbled to life.

Man, I hoped they didn't hear.

Slowly I turned the van around in the narrow farmer's lane. Soon, I was on my way.

I kept gazing into the rear-view mirror fully expecting to see them burst out of the trees and come running naked after me. But they were hobbled together. It would take them some time to figure out how to co-ordinate their walking while chained together.

It wouldn't be easy. I spoke from experience.

My foot kept pressing on the gas pedal and I kept having to ease off and slow down.

I had to act like I belonged in this vehicle. Like I was a prison guard. I yanked the cap lower on my head as I approached the dirt road that would lead to the highway. Thankfully, no one was around.

My knuckles were white as I held tight to the steering wheel. I felt woozy with fear. My legs were shaking and so was pretty much the rest of me.

I swear I almost passed out as I saw a black car whiz by just up ahead on the highway. When I came to the intersection, my mouth was so dry, that I could barely keep myself from stopping at the stop sign.

My heart crashed in my ears as I gazed left and then right. The other vehicle I'd seen was already way ahead in the distance.

I turned the van onto the highway, going the opposite way of the prison toward the city. Once I got to the city, I knew where to take it. To my old neighborhood. I'd remembered an acquaintance of my mom who knew someone who ran a chop shop.

I'll sell him the van and he'd make it disappear.

I grinned as I spied Dixon and Ashton's wallets in the tray between the seats. I knew someone who would give me a great deal of money for those radios, cop weapons, those wallets that would be filled with credit cards and ID. By the time Dixon and Ashton found help, I'd have hopped on a bus for another city in some new clothing purchased with cash.

I'd disappear.

I settled my hand upon my abdomen and smiled.

We were free.

The End

Spunky Girl Publishing Catalog

Jasmine Black
~Erotica~Without the
Romance

Here are some more Jasmine Black eBooks...

Taken by Two Cowboys

Sierra Allan works hard at her late-father's horse ranch. When her step-brother adds her handy girl services to a private auction to help raise money for the failing ranch, she figures there's no harm...but she's stunned when her services are sold to two sexy cowboys who give her an erotic way to save the ranch—submitting to their dark desires..

Taken by Three Billionaires

Billionaire friends, Liam, Theo and Elijah have just won Princess Isabella in a billionaire card game. Isabella knows exactly what the three men will want from her...she just hadn't expected to have all three of them at once!

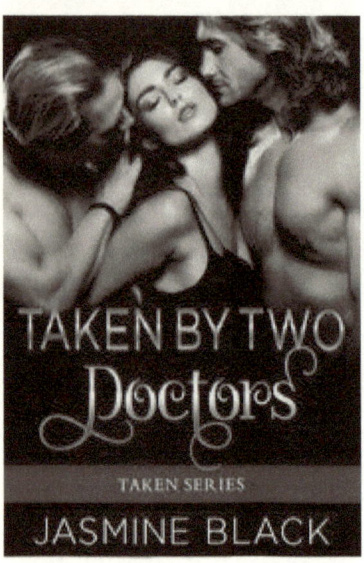

Taken by Two Doctors
A BDSM Medical Fetish Erotica Quickie MFM

Waitress Jean Spelling visits her controversial doctor once a month for
some much-needed...stress relief. She looks forward to putting her feet
up in the stirrups and enjoys Dr. Ball's naughty unconventional
treatments. This time when she arrives, she's surprised to discover that
she'll be physically examined by two doctors and they'll prescribe her
some much-needed release right there on the examination table!

eBooks in Jasmine Black's Ménage series
Taken by Three Bodyguards
Taken by Three Bikers
Taken by Three Billionaires
Taken by Three Doctors
Taken by Three Cowboys

---

eBooks in Jasmine Black's Taken series
Taken by Two Prison Guards
Taken by Two Elves
Taken by Two Mountain Men
Taken by Two Cops
Taken by Two Santas
Taken by Two Lifeguards
Taken by Two Firefighters
Taken by Two Bikers
Taken by Two Billionaires
Taken by Two Bosses
Taken by Two Cowboys
Taken by Two Personal Trainers
Taken by Two Carpenters

Jasmine Black Website ~ http://www.jasmine-black.com
Twitter ~ @blackerotica1

Jan Springer ~ Erotic Romance ~

~

Cowboys For Christmas
Cowboys Online 1 ~ Moose Ranch
Jan Springer
A Canadian Contemporary Ménage Romance m/f/m/m Series

Jennifer Jane (JJ) Watson has spent the past ten Christmases in a maximum-security prison.

The last thing she expects is to get early parole, along with a job on a remote Canadian cattle ranch serving Christmas holiday dinners to three of the sexiest cowboys she's ever met!

Rafe, Brady and Dan thought they were getting a couple of male ex-cons to help out around their secluded ranch, but instead they get an attractive and very appealing female.

In the snowbound wilds of Northern Ontario, female companionship is rare.

It's a good thing the three men like to share...

They're dominating, sexy-as-sin and they fill JJ with the hottest ménage fantasies she's ever had. Suddenly she's craving cowboys for Christmas and wishing for something she knows she can never have...a happily ever after.

---◦◦◦---

Cowboys In Her Pocket
Cowboys Online 2 ~ Moose Ranch
Jan Springer

After spending ten years in a maximum-security prison Jennifer Jane (JJ) Watson got early parole and a job on a remote Canadian cattle ranch playing housekeeper to three of the sexiest cowboys she's ever met...

Spring has finally arrived at Moose Ranch, and a single woman fresh out of prison shouldn't be experiencing scorching ménages with her three sexy-as-sin cowboys. But JJ's love for her men continues to grow as she gives into the fevered heat and scorching passions she feels for each of them.

Life is perfect.

Until her new life is tested when mysterious happenings occur on the ranch and then one of her cowboys is viciously attacked and injured. Will JJ's newfound freedom and happiness be ripped away?

Rafe, Brady and Dan never expected to find an attractive and very appealing female to help them out at their secluded ranch. But in the wilds of Northern Ontario, female companionship is rare. It's a good thing the three men like to share...

Brady, Dan and Rafe have never been happier. Their cattle ranch is flourishing and their continued desire to share the sexy woman who cares for them makes their life complete. Until danger threatens to rip everything apart...

Loving Her Cowboys
Cowboys Online 3 ~ Moose Ranch
Jan Springer

After spending ten years in a maximum-security prison Jennifer Jane (JJ) Watson got early parole and a job on a remote Canadian cattle ranch playing housekeeper to three of the sexiest cowboys she's ever met...

Her love for her cowboys continues to grow as she gives into fevered heat. But JJ's simmering restlessness explodes and she's seriously making up for lost time by pursuing her dreams. There's only one little problem. She hasn't revealed to her bosses what she's been up to while they're away tending to the cattle. She knows when they discover her secret, there will be hell to pay.

Ranchers Rafe, Dan and Brady have found the woman who completes them. She makes their secluded ranch a home-sweet-home. She's vulnerable, sweet and willing to share her bed with all three of them. But when JJ's secret is unwittingly revealed, they're stunned and angry. They figure it's time to dole out some fiery punishment in some mighty naughty ways...

———— ⋘❦⋙ ————

Cowboys In Her Heart
Cowboys Online #4

After spending ten years in a maximum-security prison, JJ gets unexpected parole and a job on a Canadian ranch serving up scrumptious dinners and lots of hot love to three of the sexiest cowboys she's ever met. Jennifer Jane "JJ" Watson has never been happier. She's going to have a baby!

Thankfully, their wilderness ranch is a nice distraction for her three sexy cowboys while she's away flying her plane. But when she's home, her dominant hunks are tending to her naughty pregnant cravings and that includes plenty of sizzling ménages.

Rafe, Brady and Dan don't much like the idea of their woman flying the Canadian skies and being at the mercy of the unpredictable

Northern Ontario weather. They would prefer having her warming their beds twenty-four seven. But she has a way of getting what she wants and right now she needs her new-found freedom.

Worst fears are realized when JJ, her friend and JJ's plane suddenly go missing and she doesn't come back home to them.

Always Her Cowboys
Cowboys Online 5 ~ Moose Ranch

1

Reader Advisory: Best to read in order. 1. Cowboys for Christmas, 2. Cowboys in Her Pocket, 3. Loving Her Cowboys, 4.Cowboys in Her Heart, 5. Always Her Cowboys. 6. Her Forever Cowboys 7. Claiming Her Cowboys

---

A Canadian Contemporary Ménage Romance m/f/m/m
Jennifer Jane (JJ) Watson has spent ten Christmases in a maximum-security prison. The last thing she expected was to get early parole, along with a job on a remote Canadian cattle ranch serving Christmas holiday dinners to three of the sexiest cowboys she's ever met!

---

1. https://janspringerauthor.files.wordpress.com/2017/11/alwayshercowboys_ebook-1new.jpg

Rafe, Brady and Dan thought they were getting male ex-cons to help out around their secluded ranch, but instead they got an attractive and very appealing female. In the snowbound wilds of Northern Ontario, female companionship is rare. It's a good thing the three men like to share...

Christmas is coming once again to Moose Ranch and with JJ's due date approaching, she's distracting herself from anxiety attacks by keeping herself ultra-busy preparing for the arrival of her baby and planning Moose Ranch's first annual Christmas party!

In having a wee baby on the way, there's a lot of stress for Brady, Rafe and Dan. Especially due to JJ's decision on having a wilderness mid-wife deliver the baby *at their secluded ranch* - with *all* of them present for the birth! But their concerns don't stop the men from showing JJ how much they love her...out of bed and in!

With wicked snowstorms, a grounded bush plane, a cheerful holiday party and a sweet baby on the way, the owners of Moose Ranch know this will be one sparkling Christmas season they won't soon forget...

PLUS: HER FOREVER COWBOYS ~ Snowy Creek Ranch #1
Cowboys Online #6
Claiming Her Cowboys ~ Moose Ranch #6 Cowboys Online #7

Risqué Girl Delights Boxed Set
(Contemporary Erotic Romance)

2

...a touch of romance, a ménage or both?

Edible Delights

Years ago Allie Masters lost herself in the scorching passion of a
ménage a trois relationship with her two bosses. In order to regain her
independence, she walked away.
Max and Nick were very fulfilled with their gorgeous assistant. The
lovemaking was breathtaking and both men willingly shared the
woman they wanted to spend the rest of their lives with. Then she left.
Now Max and Nick have decided it's time to seduce Allie back into
their lives.

Toygasm

---

2. https://janspringerauthor.files.wordpress.com/2015/02/rgdelights_box_js_3d_noshadow-1.jpg

It's a case of mistaken identity when the two owners of Sexy Toys, show up for an erotic several day photo shoot of their toys with famous nude model Cammie Creek.

Cammie believes the two hunks are the male models she's supposed to work with. Usually she doesn't mix business with pleasure, but when they're seducing her right there in front of the camera, she can't resist turning them into her own personal naughty toys.

Josh and Jode are enjoying the perks of being male models; hot lust, sizzling toys and the best pleasure they've ever had. But how will Cammie react when she discovers they're actually her bosses and not just male models?

Shy Girl

Finally free of an abusive relationship, "Shy Girl" Emma McCall sheds her inhibitions and explores her sensual side at Club Rendezvous, a club specializing in the Alternate Lifestyle.

At the club she's surprised to find Logan Masters, a sexy hunk she's secretly fantasized about since college. With Logan's help, Emma will experience her ultimate fantasy - a scorching ménage a trois.

Risqué Girl Delights Boxed Set Con't

Roman and Julietta

Her perfect lover...

Modern day pirate Julietta Black's life has always been immersed in the
violent and traditional ways of piracy. When her family's arch enemy
puts a hit out on her family, Julietta knows there's only one way to lift
the hit; she must kidnap the enemy's sexy grandson and force a union
between the two warring families. Night after night, wrapped in
Roman's strong arms, she can't deny the searing attraction blazing
between them. Nor can she deny he now holds her heart as well as her
life in his hands.

His dream angel...

When Roman Prince's mysterious captor offers him a luscious woman
to bed, fierce desire ignites, melting his usually tight self-control. Lust
quickly turns to love as he enjoys their naughty trysts more than he
should. How will he react when he discovers he's been kidnapped, not
for a ransom, but captured for his sperm?

Alpha Outlaws Boxed Set (Books 1-5 Outlaw Lovers)
5 Books!!

3

In a world gone mad...
A fast-acting virus has killed a majority of the world's female population.
With the creation of The Claiming Law, groups of men suddenly have the
right to claim a female as their sensual property and the sexy Outlaw
brothers are going to declare ownership of the women they love...any way
they can.

Jude Outlaw
When Cate Callahan learns Jude is coming home from the Terrorist
Wars and is ready to claim her under the new law—with the help of
his four brothers—she steals their boat and escapes to the high seas.
Unfortunately, her runaway bid for freedom doesn't last long.

---

3. https://janspringerauthor.files.wordpress.com/2010/07/alphaoutlaws_js_box_final.jpg

Quickly capturing his lover, Jude rekindles the flames and seduces Cate back into his bed.
But Jude holds a secret that could make him lose Cate forever...
PLUS

The Claiming
Seeking refuge from the Claiming Law, Callie Callahan hides in a deserted cabin in the Maine woods and is shocked when her ex-flame finds her. She's always craved being in Luke Outlaw's arms. Tasting him. Touching him. Taking him deeply within her. So, what's a girl to do but to delve into the sinful delights he offers.
Luke has finally reunited with the love of his life. He knows there is only one way to keep Callie safe and with him forever. He'll do it with the help of his three brothers and an assortment of naughty toys. Rekindling the flames between them, he unleashes Callie's sensual side, taking her in ways she never dreamed possible, all with the ultimate goal of introducing her to the Outlaw Lovers and The Claiming.

Alpha Outlaws Boxed Set Con't

Colter's Revenge
Revenge belongs to Dr. Colter Outlaw when he unexpectedly reunites with the beautiful woman who broke his heart during the Terrorist Wars. Capturing her, collaring her and holding her against her will, he seduces her, fills her with wicked desires and naughty cravings for a delicious ménage. Fully intent on breaking her heart and walking away, Colter's plans unravel when he submits to the carnal pleasures Ashley gives him so freely.

Colter had told her he loved her. He'd whispered promises of rescue from her life as a slave, but when he'd suddenly disappeared, she'd been devastated. Infected with a version of the X-virus that leaves Ashley Blakely sexually excited on a daily basis, she has come to Pleasure Palace to bid on a cure for her illness. She never expected her Outlaw Lover to be there and screw her plans. Nor did she expect to give him her heart and body so easily...

Tyler's Woman

For years Tyler Outlaw and his best friend, Hunter Brown, endured brutal torture and worse in an overseas terrorist prison. Finally, free of their hell, they return home intent on seducing Laurie into their erotic-filled fantasies.

Laurie Callahan has always experienced red-hot pleasure and passionate love in Tyler Outlaw's arms. But when he's pronounced MIA, presumed dead in the Terrorist Wars, Laurie's world is shattered, and her heart is broken.

Shocked to discover Tyler is alive and he's taken a male lover, Laurie is thrust into a sensual world of sizzling seductions, scorching ménages and the carnal desires that both scarred men crave. But she fears Tyler won't want her when he discovers she's not the same woman he left behind...

****READER CAUTION IS ADVISED (m/m forced scenes) ****

Resistance

In the near future, a virus has been unleashed, killing a majority of the world's female population, forcing the introduction of the Claiming Law. A law that states men have all the rights and women are sexual property claimable by groups of men.

Fugitive female...

Renegade Resistance leader Reena "Red" Wilde is in for the fight of her life when she experiences an erotic attraction to the two most dangerous men she's ever met.

Black ops assassin...

Months ago, Will "Blade" Smith spent one sizzling evening in the arms of a red-haired seductress. Now she's his next assignment. One look into her gorgeous eyes and he's wrestling his heated cravings for her all over again.

Bounty Hunter...

When Cade Outlaw nabs his bounty, sexy-as-sin Reena Wilde, his profession dictates she's hands-off. But he can't ignore the magnetic sparks between them...or that she is the biggest temptation of his life.

Resistance is futile...

After Reena escapes Cade and Will and falls prey to a band of evil hunters, she's grateful her sexy hunks come to her rescue...and in return, saves their lives. Trapped in a solitary cabin during a wicked snowstorm, she can't resist her two, well-hung studs, nor can she deny they've claimed her heart.

Many more Jasmine Black and Jan Springer eBooks, print books, audiobooks plus translated eBooks and print books can be found at http://www.janspringer.com and http://www.jasmine-black.com

Here are ways we can connect:

Jasmine Black Website at http://janspringerauthor.wordpress.com/
jasmine-black/
Jan Springer Website at http://www.janspringer.com[1]
Instagram – http://www.instagram.com/janspringerauthor
Facebook - https://www.facebook.com/janspringereroticromance
Twitter Jan Springer- https://twitter.com/janspringer @janspringer
Twitter Jasmine Black - https://twitter.com/blackerotica1
@blackerotica1
Pinterest - http://www.pinterest.com/janspringer1/
Jan's Blog - http://janspringerauthor.wordpress.com/blog-2/
Happy Reading,
Jasmine Black / Jan Springer

Don't miss out!

Visit the website below and you can sign up to receive emails whenever Jasmine Black publishes a new book. There's no charge and no obligation.

https://books2read.com/r/B-A-GIJD-SOVDC

BOOKS 2 READ

Connecting independent readers to independent writers.

www.ingramcontent.com/pod-product-compliance
Lightning Source LLC
Chambersburg PA
CBHW022040170626
46808CB00003B/1298